ex Libris

Preincarnate

Preincarnate

A NOVELLA

BY

SHAUN MICALLEF

❧

WITH TWENTY-THREE ILLUSTRATIONS
BY BILL WOOD

Published in 2010 by
Hardie Grant Books
85 High Street
Prahran, Victoria 3181, Australia
www.hardiegrant.com.au

Copyright © Shaun Micallef
Copyright illustrations © Bill Wood

National Library of Australia Cataloguing-in-Publication entry:
Author: Micallef, Shaun.
Title: Preincarnate / Shaun Micallef.
Edition: 1st ed.
ISBN: 9781740669818 (hbk.)
Dewey Number: A823.3

Cover design by Peter Long
Cover image by Alexander Nezeritis, courtesy flickr.com
Text design and page layout by Peter Long
Illustrations by Bill Wood
Edited by Janet Austin
Typeset in Adobe Caslon
Printed and bound in Australia by McPhersons Printing

10 9 8 7 6 5 4 3 2 1

For Joseph, Gabriel and Elias

*In Eternity there is no
distinction of Tenses.*

SIR THOMAS BROWNE,
RELIGIO MEDICI

Contents

I clutched my valise tightly to my chest.

THE LARGE AND LUMINOUS CLOCK
face of the otherwise lifeless Gare
d'Orsay had treacherously given the
Paris night sky two moons so that I might more
easily be seen by my enemies. Bitterly cold,
I crunched across the snow-covered Arcole
Bridge as quickly as my injury would allow,
leaving traces of blood that seemed almost
black against the white-encrusted ironwork.

Once clear of the street lamps, I clutched
my valise tightly to my chest and hobbled away
into the shadows, the shrill whistles of the
gendarmes receding with every step.

I did not know the missing man, but his
name was Alexander Pruitt.

A Preliminary Note

THE HUMAN SOUL IS A REMARKABLE thing. In simple terms, it is that sense each of us has of our Self; the awareness we have when we wake up in the morning that we are the same person we were when we went to bed the night before.

When the body that houses our soul dies, that soul is released into the Ether. Any consciousness of its previous life is erased, and the cleansed soul enters the next available newborn body. And so the Wheel of Life is given a fresh spin and the Journey to Enlightenment takes up where it left off.

In essence, it is a sensible system of recycling, and it worked quite well for aeons until the

Earth's human population started living longer. With the living hanging on to their souls and more and more people being born, the result, in market terms, was that the demand for souls quickly outstripped supply. This created all sorts of problems, not least of which was a Humanity increasingly devoid of purpose.

The soul became vulnerable to looting by unscrupulous necromancers, and some of your lesser religions started working a type of spiritual queue-jumping into their dogma. In short, a black market in souls developed. And so it was that the souls of beings other than humans were pressed into service to prevent the Wheel of Life seizing up.

This influx of sub-human souls into the Divine Plan certainly oiled the Wheel of Life, but it also made it much bigger. The Wheel of Life wound up taking so long to go round that the Journey to Enlightenment, for most people, became virtually imperceptible.

The Ether, too, had its work cut out coping with the increased multitude of souls, while ensuring all traces of past life were erased from each one. Every now and then, a Shirley MacLaine was bound to slip through.

And no longer was it just a question of processing the soul's memory. In the old days, the soul of a particularly nasty murderer might have needed three or four virtuous life cycles before all vestiges of sin were eradicated, but the modern soul of, say, an E. coli was a horse of an entirely different kettle of fish. Unicellular organisms require several billion trips through

Every now and then, a Shirley MacLaine was bound to slip through.

the Ether for their souls to be anywhere near fit enough to become one with God. The Buddhists are spot on here, and it's why the Apocalypse keeps getting postponed. If it were all just lions, fish, gorillas and other multicellular creatures, we'd have all achieved Oneness with the Grand Architect, experienced our Rapture and been mercifully blown to Kingdom Come by now. But no, Life goes on and on interminably, thanks to

4

those stubborn, hard-to-clean, microscopic organisms.

Alexander Pruitt's soul was one of the good ones though. Pure, 100 per cent Decent Human Being.

Chapter 1

**IN WHICH ALEXANDER PRUITT
CONFRONTS HIS PAST**

*7th day of March Anno Domini Iesu Christi 2005,
20:33:45 post meridiem GMT, Camden St Egham, Kent*

T ALL SEEMED FAMILIAR ENOUGH: the single bed, the dangling aeroplanes, the golliwog wallpaper, the battered bureau – but in miniature. Gulliver in Lilliput, thought Alexander as he looked around the tiny room.

He slid his suitcase between the short-looking tallboy and shrunken chest of drawers, and opened the wardrobe to a hollow jangle of empty hangers. It could easily hold a child's belongings, but was not deep enough to accommodate the clothing of a broad-shouldered 35-year-old. He decided to unpack his suitcase anyway, hanging up what he could and looking for his favourite jumper, which he couldn't find.

He caught sight of himself in the fly-specked mirror. His nose was too big, his hair was too red and his eyes were too sad.

Alexander Pruitt had never felt he belonged here. Growing up, he'd been drawn to nothing. Not to school, his friends — not even to his parents. There was no change when he became an adolescent and adult. Marrying Isabelle had been a big mistake. He'd thought that by travelling in her wake he could feed off her momentum and absorb her purpose, but instead he'd slowed her down and so she'd cut him loose.

And now he was back where he'd begun. It wasn't that he minded his life coming full circle, he just hadn't expected it to be such a small circle. He went downstairs, where at least his self-pity would have an audience.

Alexander's father had done a good job with the kitchen. By a process of canny neglect, Charlie Pruitt had allowed the original 1940s décor and fittings to age into a sort of retro-chic déshabillé. Charlie, who had undergone a comparable process but with a much less fashionable result, pottered about collecting the tea things and blathering away at a volume more attuned to his own malfunctioning hearing aid than the regular workings of a human ear.

Charlie was bigger than his son. Burly. In his youth he might have been considered handsome. He had a snub nose, big jolly cheeks and a face used to smiling. His thinning hair had never been red, and was once probably blond. Alexander didn't take after his father at all.

'Well, it's nice to have you back,' Charlie continued. 'I know it couldn't have been pleasant but there's nout you can do but look for the silver lining. Gawd, your mum was dead when I was your age – at least Bella's alive and happy, eh?'

'Yes, I'm sure she and the chap she ran off with are delirious with joy,' observed Alexander with the parched wit that had made him the man to avoid at social gatherings.

Charlie shuffled out of the kitchen, across the draughty hallway and into the living room, with Alexander following superfluously behind.

The old man had once been a young man, of course, and the young man had once been a sculptor. The years had passed and Charlie had a family to support, and so the artist had become an artisan, whittling Western features onto Japanese mannequins for a shop-fittings importer. He was very good, and sometimes he would fashion his late wife's countenance onto the dummies, just for the hell of it. Alexander could still remember the day when, as a boy, he'd been walking down the high street and seen his dead mother looking out at him from a store-front window.

Half a pot of weak tea later, Charlie was still holding court. Alexander held his father's rheumy gaze and nodded occasionally, a rictus of a smile on his face. Less than an hour back home and he'd already disengaged. He pondered the conker tree in the front garden, visible through the grubby front curtains. It had been too small to climb when he was a child, and now that it was of sufficient height and robustness he was too big to play on it.

A gaunt figure dressed in black was standing outside the house, squinting as he checked and re-checked a slip of paper. He had already passed the conker tree a couple of times, walking up and down the street, but

Alexander hadn't given much thought to him. Now that the man had come to a stop outside the house, Alexander shifted in his seat. Charlie turned as the front gate creaked open and the stranger started up the garden path.

'Bit late for visitors,' muttered the old man, pulling himself out of the chair.

Alexander was on his feet too. Something about the man in black made him feel uncomfortable. From time to time he would

He couldn't make out the stranger's face
through the mottled glass.

get this feeling about certain people or things. Nothing you would call a premonition; just a sort of dread feeling in the pit of his stomach.

Charlie was already in the hall when the door chimed, barking that he was coming. Peering through the mottled front window, Alexander tried to get a closer look at the man standing on the front porch. He couldn't quite make out the stranger's face but he noticed that his clothes were old. Not in age – they looked quite new, in fact – but in fashion. A silver watch chain gleamed out from the man's black waistcoat, stretching tight across his belly as if it were holding the two sides of his body together. The slip of paper he'd been consulting was held in a gloved hand. The other, now ungloved, was tipping a hat to Charlie as the door opened.

The man's softly spoken words were muffled but his Scottish accent was oddly familiar and, while Alexander couldn't make out what his father was saying either, it was clear from his tone that Charlie was begging off. Perhaps the man was selling something.

Then the stranger looked over at the window and an electric chill raced from

Alexander's neck to the top of his head. It was a cold and inquisitive look. The man nodded hello and then turned back to Charlie, who reluctantly welcomed him inside. A moment later, Charlie appeared at the living room door.

'Alexander, there's someone I think you should meet.'

If Alexander knew anything about his father it was that he never entertained. Most of his parents' friends had stopped coming around after Alexander's mother had died, and now no-one ever dropped in. And besides, this fellow didn't seem to be a friend.

'This is Doctor Moray,' announced Charlie with an unusual degree of formality.

Alexander walked over to shake hands with the doctor, who seemed enormously tall, perhaps a touch under seven feet. Charlie lingered uncertainly by the door.

'You have no idea how wonderful it is to see you again, lad,' said the giant intruder, smiling with affection at Alexander, who looked to his father for clarification.

'Doctor Moray delivered you when you were a baby,' Charlie explained.

'Ah, well, I knew the name but couldn't place the face,' quipped Alexander nervously. He'd never heard of Doctor Moray.

The good doctor made a noise that might have been a laugh. Charlie urged the man to take a seat in the good chair and, after draping his coat over the arm of the weathered Harlequin wingback and perching his hat on top, he did so, his hands folded neatly in his lap. Doctor Moray then motioned to the couch opposite him and Alexander dutifully sat, thinking how strange it was to be offered a seat in your own home.

Charlie remained standing, perhaps out of respect for their guest. Doctor Moray beamed at the young man before him, drinking him in. Then a serious expression clouded his face and he leaned forward, resting his chin in his hands and his elbows on his bony knees, looking a little too much like a hungry praying mantis.

'Before you were born, Alexander, your mother and father came to see me. At that time I worked at a fertility clinic ...'

This was news to Alexander. He looked over to Charlie, who nodded and with a tilt of his head indicated that his son should turn his attention back to their guest.

'Your mother was very keen to have you,' continued the doctor, picking at some imaginary lint on his knee. 'Your father too, of course.'

'We were having troubles,' Charlie chipped in.

'There were complications,' continued Doctor Moray. 'The procedures we used were …' and here the doctor chose his next word very carefully, '… *unconventional*.'

If a distant wolf had been nearby it would have howled.

Doctor Moray unfurled himself from the good chair and walked over to Alexander. He stooped to place a comforting speckled hand on his shoulder.

'There's nothing to worry about,' he smiled. 'I'm just checking up on the children who were produced by this procedure to see if they're well. Sometimes there are problems that only manifest themselves in later years – but then there are always problems in later years, aren't there?' A bubble of inappropriate laughter accompanied these last few words.

'I guess,' shrugged Alexander. 'What exactly do you mean by "unconventional"?' Actually,

Alexander had been more discomfited by the word 'produced'. It made him sound like a piece of extruded plastic.

Moray shot Charlie a quick look and then, just as quickly, locked his now flinty eyes on Alexander.

'Nothing to worry about,' he repeated in a tone that suggested the opposite.

'But there have been problems, haven't there? Or you wouldn't be here,' Alexander persisted. 'And how did you know I'd moved back home?'

Dead air filled the room as Charlie cleared his throat and rubbed at a mark on the Axminster with the toe of his shoe, while Doctor Moray studied a dusty light fitting.

'It's just a check up, Al,' said Charlie, finally breaking the silence.

Alexander was keen to get this over with. His father hadn't called him Al in twenty-five years.

'All right then, if it's just a check up.'

'Excellent,' smiled Doctor Moray. It was a broader smile, proving all his other smiles had not been genuine – and revealing a horrible crowded jumble of yellow teeth.

Chapter 2

IN WHICH A SECRET IS REVEALED TO THE MAN FROM ST IVES

*8th day of March Anno Domini Iesu Christi 2005,
13:45:02 post meridiem GMT, St Ives, Hertfordshire*

 DID NOT KNOW ALEXANDER Pruitt, but because of him, within six months, I would find myself in a crypt beneath the Masonic Lodge Rosslyn St Clair (No. 606, Edinburgh), using a tyre iron to prise the lid off a sepulchre. Inside I would discover not only a perfectly preserved 350-year-old body, but secreted in the stone base of the sepulchre, a set of instructions for the body's revivification. A few days later, and I'd be limping at speed over the Arcole Bridge in Paris, clutching my bleeding leg.[1]

---

1. Six months later still, I'd be arguing with my editor over whether we should include this paragraph as it's a bit

Truth be told, I'm far more at home crumpled in a tweedy heap deep within the folds of a much-loved and cracked leather chair. Mine happens to be next to the large upstairs bow window of the Boar's Club, overlooking the lovingly tonsured hedge maze that is the centrepiece of St Ives College cloisters. The Boar's Club has been my refuge since I became Rector of St Ives some eighteen months ago.

Traditionally, the post of Rector is an honorary one, bestowed on minor celebrities and other folk of dim and passing notoriety. I, however, decided to take the Student Union at their word, and moved up to Hertfordshire and into an abandoned cottage just within the college grounds. Once ensconced, I helped students with their problems, offered sage advice to befuddled dons and generally wandered about taking advantage of the perks of my office, which included membership at the Boar's.

It was from the Boar's Club that the First XI had rallied at my urging to protest their

confusing. In the end, we decided to keep it and lose the one about badgers.

A damned good likeness too; I had to look twice.

shoddy college-supplied flannels (unchanged since Edward IV wore them) and from whence, incandescently incensed, they'd marched as one with placards to the Vice-Chancellor's rooms and promptly burned him in effigy (a damned good likeness too; I had to look twice). Generally, however, the club was a hidey-hole to retire to with a good brandy and a fine cigar; somewhere to chat with freckled old men, guffaw at antique jokes and muse on life, or meld, half-forgotten, into the darkly stained woodwork.

The *cause célèbre* that had prompted my invitation from the Student Union to become Rector had been an unseasonably warm review from the *Times Literary Supplement* for my first excursion into print, *Citizen Cromwell*, a painstakingly researched account of the rather dull private life of England's Lord Protector during the mid-1600s. Inspiration for my much-anticipated second book was proving somewhat elusive.

❧

SO THERE I'D BEEN EARLIER THIS MORNING, nestled in my cracked leather chair at the Boar's, happily lost in the racing form, when from a triangular shaft of sunlit dust had stepped Una, my impossibly beautiful research assistant. Held in her delicate hand was an envelope.

'You reminded me to remind you about this, Professor,' she breathed, before leaving me to myself; a generous bequest.

The envelope was addressed to me in my own handwriting. As I distractedly tore it

open, a scrap of paper slipped from its slim
and pliant gullet.

Fox and Grapes Hotel –
8th March AD 2005.
Afternoon. Old man.
UPSET!!!
(c.f. H.G. Wells???)

Four years earlier, Una had come across these
words and the reference to today's date while
fact hunting for my Cromwellian opus. They
appeared in the journal of a seventeenth-
century physician's apprentice, now housed in
the Boolean Library.

When Una had first brought the words
to my attention, I'd found them curious and
had scrawled a note to myself to keep track of
the date. I found things even curiouser now
that I was sitting in a banquette at the Fox
and Grapes, nursing a beer, and an old guy was
sliding into the booth opposite me, his eyes a
little rheumier than normal.

I sucked the head off my pony of
Kristallweizen and tried to look as if I weren't

sitting there as a result of a 350-year-old diary entry.

'Wazzup, old-timer?' I asked, bridging the generation gap and lightening the mood to helium level.

The old man mumbled something at the table and shook his head.

'You sure?'

'I'm fine,' he said, a little louder this time.

'You don't seem fine.'

'Well, I am fine.' He was looking up now, his misty eyes boiling at me.

'I appreciate that and I don't want to pry,' I lied. 'I'm just saying it seems there's something wrong and ... you know, maybe I can help.'

'Well, firstly, there ain't nout anyone can do,' he gulped, helping himself to a stray chip from the remains of my *frittura mista*. 'And secondly, there ain't nout wrong in the first place.'

I was getting nowhere and slowly.

'So, what's—' I began, trying a different approach but abandoning it by the end of the second word.

The old man stole another chip.

'Look, you're obviously upset ...' I tried

again. 'I'm a good listener and sometimes a good listener is just what you need.'

'For a good listener, you talk an awful lot,' cracked the old man, leaving half a smile on his face.

I pushed the bowl over.

The old man was a regular. Big guy. About seventy years of age, maybe more. Receding sandy hair. Liver spots on his hands. Worker's hands, I thought: rough and ingrained with something. Paint? Resin? He had a blanched look. Like an almond. I made a mental note: *tradesman*. Then I listened.

Chapter 3

IN WHICH ALEXANDER PRUITT MEETS HIS MAKER

8th day of March Anno Domini Iesu Christi 2005,
08:15:12 ante meridiem GMT, Harley Street, London

HE RADIO HADN'T WORKED FOR two years, but the clatter of the untuned engine in the Hillman Minx helped mask the uneasy silence between father and son during the drive into town for Alexander's medical appointment.

While idling at a red light, the wreck's noise reduced to only a few squeaks and grinds, the old man turned to his son.

'It was my idea,' said Charlie. 'I was in my cups one night at the Lodge, and Doctor Moray and I fell to talking. He told me on the QT about this new procedure. It wasn't *actually* legal back then, you see ...'

'Green light, Dad.'

With a grunt, Charlie forced the gearstick into first and the car lurched uncertainly into the junction.

'There was a lot of talk about it in the papers – will they legalise it, won't they legalise it? But, given your mum was forty, we couldn't really afford to wait, now could we?'

Alexander watched the rows of shops dawdle past as the Hillman gathered what speed it could. Charlie's question might not have been rhetorical but it didn't matter. Alexander didn't feel he was really there anyway.

❧

DOCTOR MORAY'S ROOMS WERE A CLEAN and neat arrangement, the white walls covered with pin boards festooned with photographs of babies. Thank-you cards crowded the receptionist's counter, jostling with flowers, ceramic figures and brochures. Also on the counter was a small, intricately engraved brass bell, its handle shaped like a Rosy Cross. The round, bespectacled woman on the other side of the counter had to half-stand in order to be seen.

'Just take a seat. The doctor will see you presently,' she said to Alexander with a professional smile that vanished the moment she sat back down. Alexander did as he was told, all the while half-wishing he was with his father, who'd popped down to the Fox and Grapes to steady his nerves.

There were two other people in the waiting room, both of them women. One was heavily pregnant with a well-fed, self-satisfied look about her; the other was bird-like, a worried expression flitting about her pinched features. Both of them looked up from their Dead Princess magazines with annoyance when Doctor Moray beckoned Alexander into his office ahead of them.

The examination was thorough enough: reflexes, eyesight, hearing, blood tests, X-rays, weight, height and a urine sample. Doctor Moray took notes, peered at Alexander through various instruments, pointed beams of light at him, nodded a lot and made humming noises, but he didn't look at Alexander-as-Alexander (as opposed to Alexander-as-examination-subject) until after the last result had been jotted down on a pink card

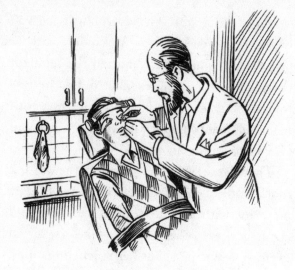

The examination was thorough enough.

and slipped into a manila folder. That slightly unsettling affectionate look from the night before returned as Moray sat back and gave his patient a dilapidated grin.

'You're in tip-top splendid health, lad,' he enthused, his accent enjoying the trip through sibilant and plosive consonants. 'You're ready ...'

Alexander bent to retie the laces on his trainers, refusing to look up at the hanging sentence.

'Let me ask you something,' Moray wheedled in his soft Scottish lilt, washing his hands in the sink behind his desk. 'Have you ever felt as though you didn't quite belong here?'

Now Alexander looked up. 'Do you mean here right now in this office, or here in this life?'

Moray chuckled, and taking a silver key from his watch chain he opened a cabinet above the sink.

'I ask you this because it's not uncommon to experience a little bit of ennui when you hit your mid-thirties. And also because – in your case – it's perfectly understandable.'

Doctor Moray removed a small black velvet box from the cabinet.

'I guess I am a little jaded with my lot,' said Alexander, watching the doctor closely. 'But it's just the way I am. Lots of people get divorced, and I just haven't found out what I want to do yet, you know, job-wise ...'

Moray nodded as he sat on the edge of his desk, absent-mindedly turning the little box over and over in his hands.

'But, you know ...' continued Alexander, his eyes inevitably drawn to the black box, 'it's not really ennui, which is a sort of boredom with everything, isn't it? What I've got is – I guess it's a sort of *disconnectedness* with everything.'

Moray finally rested the black velvet box on his knee.

'I'm very hard to surprise,' Alexander continued, his eyes flitting between the doctor and his little box. 'You know, I was almost hit by a car once and I didn't flinch. It was almost like … it was like I wasn't actually there.'

Alexander didn't know it but he'd hit the nail on the head.

Moray gave a half smile and opened the mysterious box to produce an alarmingly large syringe – the hypodermic needle was probably five inches long – filled with a glittering turquoise fluid.

'Yes, well, shall I fix up the account at reception...' stammered Alexander as he quickly rose from his chair.

It was the last thing he could remember doing before he blacked out.

∽

THOSE WHO HAVE COME BACK FROM the brink often speak of being drawn towards a bright light, hovering for a moment above their dead body as they watch the surgeons trying desperately to revive them or their loved ones sobbing inconsolably over them. Though they wish for nothing more than to be drawn into the light, a force far greater deems that it is not yet their time, and they suddenly find themselves back in their body, gasping their way into a second chance at Life. The body will not give up its ghost until it is good and ready (and vice versa).

Every living thing on Earth is a purpose-built receiver for its own unique signal, the soul. While there is even a hint of life left in the corporeal antenna, the signal will not leave it. In the event of violent and life-threatening trauma – say, a heart attack, car accident or being injected with a lethal dose of Gaboon adder poison – the body suddenly stops working and there is a moment when the soul jolts away from its receiver. This is the delicate, immeasurable instant between Life and Death. And this is what happened to Alexander Pruitt the moment Doctor Moray stuck him with the needle.

Normally, Alexander's soul would have hovered in this out-of-body stasis for an attosecond before making straight for the Ether.

But because Alexander was a twig,[2] things were far outside the realm of normal. When he died, for a 116-millionth of a second, Alexander Pruitt was exactly the same age a certain Richard Cromwell had been when he died in 1657. Two unique souls leaving two identical bodies, either side of a vast but ultimately meaningless chasm of Time. A fraction of a millionth of a second more or less, and it might not have worked.

Because Richard Cromwell died over a number of weeks from injuries he'd received in the Battle of Worcester, his weakened soul didn't hover over his body for an attosecond as Alexander's did. It packed its bags and disappeared into the cleansing Ether quick smart – only to be replaced in that same instant by the frantically Life-seeking soul of Alexander Pruitt.

It was a metaphysical juggling act for which Doctor Moray had spent well over his entire life preparing. And as he stood over Alexander's inert body, breathless at what he had done, he would never know if in murdering a twig[3] he had saved the life of its host.

---

2. I'll explain later.
3. I said I'd explain later.

Chapter 4

IN WHICH DOCTOR MORAY MUST DIE

12th day of September Anno Domini Iesu Christi 2005, 22:12:00 post meridiem GMT, Île de la Cité, Paris

 DID NOT KNOW DOCTOR ROBERT Fenwick Aloysius Moray but I had read about him.[4] He came to prominence just as the Commonwealth of England gave way to the return of the Monarchy, when blinkered thought gave way to Enlightenment,

---

4. He was many things to many people. A proud son of Edinburgh, a colonel in the army of Louis XIII, a friend and confidant to Cardinal Richelieu, a General of Ordinance in the Covenanter Army, a knight in the Court of Charles I, a soldier in Cardinal Mazarin's army, the first President of the Royal Society and the first Freemason ever to appear in official records. He was also, most famously, instrumental in securing the Restoration of Charles II. Most importantly of all, he was the last person to see Alexander Pruitt the day he disappeared.

and Magic yielded to Science.

But here's the curious thing – Doctor Moray was born in 1609. Alexander Pruitt was born more than 350 years later. These two men, who should never have met, first did so in 1970, and again in the year 2005. They would next meet in 1657, and then again 231 years later in 1888. And while Doctor Moray would live to be 412 years of age, Alexander Pruitt would die in the year 2005 at the age of thirty-five – twice. On both occasions he would be murdered – and on both occasions it would be at the hand of Doctor Moray.

֍

THE PAIN, ROUNDING ON ME IN WAVES a few hours ago, has dulled. And despite the fact that I've not slept at all during the past three days, I remain wide-eyed. When you've been chased all over Paris by assassins, it's a little difficult to turn off the adrenaline. I've made good use of my insomnia though and, having checked into a hotel on the Île de la Cité, I laid out before me the research I've collated over the last few months, so that I might make sense of it all.

If you were to retrace my most recent steps back across the Seine to the Left Bank, past the Gare d'Orsay and down the hill to the Salférino métro station, onto a south-bound train to change at Montparnasse, onto the *ligne* 4 to get off after three stops and pop directly across the road, you would find yourself, as I did, at the entrance of the Ossuary of Denfert-Rochereau. And you would see that the lock has been smashed.

This was not my doing. Had you been passing just two hours earlier at eight in the evening, you would have seen a fist of gendarmes attacking the door to the ossuary with a metal ram. Emanating from the bowels of the Catacombs, you might have heard the faint ratchet-crackle of semi-automatic gunfire. From the safety of your vantage point, as opposed to racing about in the underground tunnels, screaming, as I was, you would have also seen the policemen engulfed in an insistent plume of smoke as the front door gave way.

One of the older gendarmes, a veteran of many campaigns – he'd manned a water cannon at the barricades in '68 – had called back the younger police officers, urging them

Belching out through the door and
into the street in a deafening curl.

to take refuge behind the wrought-iron pissoir across the road. It had proven to be sound advice. As the cold Parisian night air was sucked inside the building, it instantly found its way down the many corridors to feed the great inferno raging below. From the resultant gulp of oxygen was born a giddy fireball that swirled its way back to the surface in a rush, belching out through the door and into the street in a deafening curl, incinerating a police car and shattering windows all along the rue de la Butte.

Before the fire that destroyed it that night, the Ossuary of Denfert-Rochereau had been quite the tourist attraction.

Fortunately, I had a map.

The Masonic symbols I could see etched into the tunnel supports corresponded exactly with those on the map drawn by Sir Arthur Conan Doyle over a hundred years earlier. I had liberated the precious document from a private collection of Sir Arthur's memorabilia on loan to the National Library, no easy task I might add. I had needed a formal letter of recommendation to be granted access, and the fact that part of the collection had then disappeared and now no longer exists may test my relationship with Professor Shore of Cambridge University – should it ever amount to anything more than me forging his signature.

The map was thought to have been concocted by Conan Doyle while writing his first Sherlock Holmes story, *A Study in Scarlet*. But I knew better.

cont. from p. 23

a large tripe-like creature. Inside, heaped into ramparts five feet high and twenty deep, throughout the unending Catacombs that stretch like tendrils under Paris herself, are the bones of seven million souls. The Catacombs were originally a matrix of quarries, but sometime in the 1700s it was decided that, for reasons of public health, the cemeteries of the city should be emptied and what was left of the bodies be stacked as artistically as possible in the thousands of damp limestone hollows. In these niches, interconnected by tunnels, which were themselves accessible by secret passages leading to and from the sewers (and, of all things, the Paris métro!), are the bones of the likes of the Comte de Mirabeau, François Rabelais and Madame de Pompadour etc, mingled with those of simple peasants. The entire contents of the Cimetière des Innocents and the Église St-Paul St-Louis alone are arranged in a single 26-kilometre stretch according only to bone type. And don't forget to visit our kiosk!

CIMETIÈRE DES INNOCENTS ET ÉGLISE ST-PAUL-ST-LOUIS

Arthur Conan Doyle was a Mason, and while his biographers contended that he never took it too seriously, the truth was he had been an ardent Mason but his passion for the Brotherhood had diminished following his meeting with Doctor Moray in 1888 –

the very year a string of particularly grisly murders occurred in London's Whitechapel area. It was Conan Doyle's innocent role in reviving Doctor Moray, his horror at what he had unleashed, and his subsequent pursuit and apprehension of this madman that would inform his great body of work over the coming decades. Professor Moriarty, the diabolical nemesis of Sherlock Holmes, was inspired by Moray, a man whose unspeakable crimes haunted Conan Doyle till the end of his days. If only Conan Doyle had handed the doctor over to the police, instead of allowing him to slip back into the hands of the Brotherhood, Alexander Pruitt would never have been murdered.

Mind you, Alexander would not have been born, either.[5]

I traipsed down the time-worn stone steps, a dog-eared piece of parchment in one hand, deluxe Maglite7 quartz piezoelectric torch in the other. In the canvas bag slung over my shoulder I carried a wooden stake and mallet,

---

5. I swear to you I will explain all this at some point. And no, I haven't forgotten about the twig business.

my valise filled with research papers and an egg salad sandwich I'd bought from a vending machine on the ferry to Calais.

The ossuary had only one mausoleum, secreted at the very centre of the Catacombs. The crypt I sought featured a prominent five-pointed star – or pentangle – a polygon favoured by Doctor Moray. I'd read that inside the crypt was a casket made entirely of black mica, with no handles or fittings. Apparently, the only way to open the coffin was to apply pressure to certain equidistant points at precisely the same moment. Sir Arthur had written that it would take three men to do it.

My eyes slowly adjusted to the gloom. There it was. Under a crude halo of shimmering stalactites, surrounded by wooden barrows of skeletal remains: a simple oblong slab, sleek and, even now, boldly futuristic. I could scarcely move. My lips went dry and, as the echoes of my footsteps faded, all I could hear was the thumping of my heart.

The crypt was by far the coldest place in the Catacombs. Far colder too than the crypt in Edinburgh, but then Doctor Moray's interment in the Denfert-Rochereau had not been as long as Alexander's in the Lodge Rosslyn St Clair, and the liquid oxygen had not begun to dissipate. Spared the need to provide the isometric niceties required by Masonic tradition, I began chopping away at the casket with my stake and mallet, splintering the lid until it easily gave way.

Inside, the body of Doctor Robert Moray lay encased in a smooth white metal skin, his metabolic rate slowed so it was barely detectable. The gas held in the frosty pipes running up and down the length of Moray's vacuum-sealed jacket kept his body's core temperature low enough to inhibit decay, while a series of small Leyden jars dispatched just enough dielectrical energy to keep his heart and brain active. The large golden shell-shaped device that fed the thin tubes to Moray's throat was affixed over his chest and held fast by belted buckles. It was a beautiful device. Jules Verne would have been proud of it, yet even he – bold visionary that he was – could not have imagined the purpose for which it had been designed.

It was this curious machine that held the glittering turquoise fluid that arrested time as

Robert Moray knew it and injected it, when required, directly into his carotid artery. Too much or too little and he would die. After so many hundreds of years, his body craved it. Perhaps it was this that had driven him mad.

There was nothing for it. Moray had to be destroyed.

I placed the tip of my stake over the golden shell and raised my mallet high, dramatically holding the pose for the benefit of a row of sightless sockets peering up at me from a design on the floor. Then my mobile started to ring, and the crypt resounded to the polyphonic strains of the *SpongeBob SquarePants* theme.

I quickly hammered away at Moray's chest, each blow glancing off the impregnable metal. Then I fumbled at the buckles, attempting to loosen the machine so I might dash it to the floor. Suddenly a skull in the heart-shaped array of tibias on the wall behind me exploded as tracer bullets ripped from an M16.

'Cease and desist this profane desecration at once!' ordered a voice.

From a hollow in the wall stepped a hooded monk, a large 'R' emblazoned on the left breast of his cassock, a semi-automatic assault rifle resting on his hip and, most alarmingly as it turned out, a lit cigarette dangling from his lip. The gas leak did the rest.

∽

'FLIGHT LIEUTENANT COCONUT MCGILLICUTTY?' came a voice, together with a knock.

It took me a moment to remember that I hadn't given my real name when I'd checked into the hotel. I looked up from my papers, swung myself off the bed and limped over to the door.

'Hello?'

My voice was cracked and thin from my operatic screaming in the ossuary earlier that evening.

'Room service, monsieur.'

I left the chain on, and opening the door a peep I clocked the maroon livery of the Hotel Malte bellboy. I also caught a whiff of the hamburger and chips I'd ordered. That clinched it. I was more than happy to risk another murder attempt if it meant I could eat a little something first. I noted the bellboy's nametag (François) and unhooked the chain.

François wheeled in his trolley and removed the stainless-steel cloche with an eroded flourish, then stood there in crumpled anticlimax, the palm of his hand flipped out expectantly.

'Thank you, François,' I said, still holding the door open.

There followed a half-hearted Mexican stand-off between François and me as we exchanged nods and smiles and some throat clearing. Eventually François gave up on his tip and slumped out of the room.

I demolished the hamburger first. This seemed fair, given it tasted like it had been condemned. *Steak haché au sauce à la ciboulette*, indeed! The chips weren't much better. You'd think the French would be able to make decent French fries.[6] They were like some weird, elongated *pommes noisettes*. The last decent bowl of chips I'd eaten had been back in the Fox and Grapes over six months before,

---

6. *Actually, French fries were invented in Belgium. Ed.*
Yes, but Belgium is part of the EU, isn't it? Auth.
And? Ed.
Well, if both France and Belgium are part of the EU, then technically … you know. Auth.
No, I don't know. Ed.
I'll email you the Wikipedia ref. Auth.

when I'd promised Charlie I'd look into the disappearance of his son.

Finding Alexander Pruitt had been easy. Even transporting him across the English Channel had not proved to be as difficult as I'd thought.

Chapter 5

IN WHICH A STITCH IN TIME SAVES ONE

23rd day of October Anno Domini Iesu Christi 1657, noonish,[7] Huntingdon, East Anglia

O-ONE WAS MORE SURPRISED than Doctor Moray when Richard Cromwell's eyes fluttered open and Alexander Pruitt looked out – not even Alexander himself, who, understandably, wasn't quite sure what was going on.

Richard Cromwell had been given up for dead. Since receiving his fatal injuries several days before, he'd been doped to the gills on valerian. Nothing had worked to save him: the leeches, the blowing of smoke into his ears, the fasting and sweating, the trance dancing; not even the

---

7. It's hard to be exact, as the Masons are yet to build the Royal Observatory at Greenwich and invent Mean Time.

more sensible measures Doctor Moray had been able to introduce, such as administering water of horsetail or dressing Richard's wounds with *oyl omphacine*. The various doctors, alchemists, magicians, charlatans and politicians gathered about Richard's bedside had been at a loss – until this miracle.

The really weird thing was that as Alexander looked around the room, he had the strangest feeling of déjà vu.

✧

AS ANY THEOLOGIAN WELL VERSED IN both Coptic antiquity and Augustinian philosophy will tell you, it is the inferior processes of the human mind that give Time the linear shape with which we tend to grasp it. First, we have the Future, which exists as an *expectation*. Then the Future becomes the Present, and is an *experience*. Finally, the Present moves into the Past and exists as a *memory*.

The truth, however, is that everything happens at once: the future, the past and the now all occur simultaneously. It's also true that experiencing the future, the past or the present as an *expectation, memory* or *experience* may not

Alexander had the strangest feeling of déjà vu.

necessarily occur in that order – or even in that combination. Once we are freed from our mind's inferior processes, a *past event* can be apprehended in the *present*, a *future event* can be recalled as a *memory*, something actually in the process of being *experienced* may seem like an *expectation*, and so on ad confusio.

According to some obscure books I've read, such apparently nonsensical apprehensions, recollections and/or experiences are known as the Six Unknowable Permutations, of which déjà vu is the best known. These moments, fleeting and quickly forgotten, occur when our inferior minds start working properly, if only for a dazzling instant. It is only in these rare flashes that we truly see the Reality of Life.

Unfortunately, this sort of cosmic awareness can never be afforded us on a permanent basis or there would be dire consequences. Any longer than a couple of seconds, and there would be a certain amount of head-exploding of the type featured in David Cronenberg's *Scanners*. What had seemed so unconvincing in 1981 turns out to be completely accurate.

Our divine make-up is such that the ability of our inferior minds to cope with the Reality of Life only gets switched to the *on* position on the Eve of Armageddon. According to my research, the exact moment is just after the Earth gives up its dead and just before the Rapture. Until then, our brains are on *stand-by*. It is only very occasionally, when some people get switched to that halfway position between *on* and *off*, that you can hear a crackle and smell the burning fuse wire that is déjà vu.

I appreciate that none of this reads quite as elegantly as the work of St Augustine, but in my defence I would like to point out that, as far as I know, St Augustine did not attempt to write any of his books with a bullet in his leg.

Chapter 6

IN WHICH DOCTOR MORAY SEES THE SHAPE
OF THINGS TO COME

*23rd day of October Anno Domini Iesu Christi 1657,
still noonish, Huntingdon, East Anglia*

UT, OF COURSE, IN THE PALE SHADOW of a now fast-receding alternate history, Richard Cromwell *did* die.

Moray looked up and out of his reverie and saw that Oliver Cromwell had entered the room. Parting the canopy bed curtains to look upon the broken body of his son, Cromwell's voice had a tinge of hope, even though he had surely been told the sad news. As Lord Protector of the Commonwealth of England, he was not used to defeat. 'Robert,' he said, turning to the physician, 'what can be done?'

Moray pursed his lips and looked down. He picked up a *gonjay* from the tray beside him, regarded it as if he didn't know quite what it was, then gently replaced it. There was no need for an answer. Both men knew there was nout that could be done.

Cromwell made his way to the oriel window and looked out over Huntingdon as a light rain spat upon the thin panes of variegated glass. He fingered the ivy that had made its way inside, having climbed up the outside wall, around the stone lion corbels and through the small gap between the crumbling grout and window frame. 'A most insistent plant, Robert,' observed Cromwell. 'Do you know Castle Urquhart?'

'I do,' answered Moray. He had lived there as a boy.

Cromwell ran his thumb over the waxy surface of a leaf. 'I brought back a cutting from the eastern wall for Elizabeth. A keepsake, you see.' He turned and smiled a little. 'It was my last campaign up north.'

Moray joined Cromwell at the window and took in the rolling hills. Theirs had been an uneasy alliance these past few weeks. Moray was a man of both science and magic, and had been a keen supporter of the now headless and dead Charles I. Cromwell was a Christmashating, non-dancing, wart-festooned Puritan, and no fan of the Chemistry Set, but he had needed Moray and his lot to save Richard. Self-interest has a way of making men very broadminded.

'Urquhart was sacked and burned a few years ago,' observed Moray, not without bitterness.

Cromwell nodded. 'And the ivy-laden walls with it, no doubt.'

'Aye,' mused Moray.

'Yet it survives,' said Cromwell, fingering the hard edge of the leaf, his smile dimming. 'Part of your home … living on part of mine.'

⁂

BICYCLES WERE FORBIDDEN IN THE seventeenth century. The Puritans had deemed that anything with wheels that was not pulled by a horse was a vanity and had to be burned. Teetering pyres of wooden bicycles blazed all over England. Thousands perished.

Doctor Moray had ignored the decree and hidden his dandy-horse up a tree in a copse near his home. The penalty for riding an outlawed velocipede was severe – beheading followed by forty lashes and a fine of £1, a not terribly well-thought-out bit of drafting from the Rump Parliament – but Moray paid it no heed. At night, even when the moon was full and he was plainly visible, he would dislodge his bicycle from atop its hideaway conifer with a well-aimed lump of coal, jump in the saddle and pedal home, singing the following ditty at the top of his lungs (which was also forbidden):

> *Oh, hi-diddley-dee – Huzzah!*
> *I'm a bicycle ridin' man.*
> *No law in the land*
> *Nor constable's hand*
> *Can stay me or cause me to stand.*
>
> *For I don't give a fig*
> *For the Puritan's jig*
> *'Round the bicycle fire that they fan.*
> *So I'll move up and down*
> *Traversing the ground*
> *I'm a bicycle ridin' maaaaaaaaaaaaaaaaaaaan!*

Whether it was the heady thrill of illegality or the privet hawk-moth he inhaled during the rather elongated final word of the last verse, Moray wasn't concentrating on the road when he pedalled home that night. He hit a badger and veered madly onto the verge and through a hedge. Branches tore at his clothes and robbed him of his wig as he trundled blindly down an embankment and into a ditch that caught fast his front wheel and catapulted him a good fifteen feet into the air. After two somersaults and a half aerial turn of the type that would one day be made famous by the Flying Wallendas, the good doctor landed upside down with a sickening *boing*, in the middle of a clearing not far from a straw hut with a smoking zig-zag chimney.

The privet hawk-moth he inhaled.

It had been years since Moray had visited these parts, but he recognised at once the toothless old woman smoking a pipe at the window. She was cackling at him. He leapt up and dusted the back of his coat with an affected show of nonchalance, looking about and nodding with approval, as if the preceding callisthenics had been his intended method of arrival.

The doctor slapped his ribs and gave an audible intake of breath through his teeth. 'Ah yes, nothing like an evening constitutional in the bracing night air!' he announced to no-one in particular and then, rather unconvincingly, pretended suddenly to notice the harridan in the hut.

The hag was hanging out of her window like a Punch and Judy puppet, her arms dangling uselessly as she heaved with laughter.

'Ah, Widow Makepeace – a delightful evening, is it not?' observed the dishevelled doctor.

It was a well-known fact that the Widow Makepeace was a witch. Witches, like bicycles, were forbidden by the Lord Protector – although, it must be said, there the similarity ended. The people of Huntingdon kept the location of this particular witch a secret from the Witchfinder-General and his fearsome deputies, for the Widow was considered by most to be a *good* witch. She could cure just about anything with a clove of garlic or a gnat's coccyx, made the most delightful sugared almond treats for the children and had once brought a giraffe back to life by shooting lightning out of her nose. In any case, these days the Government was more concerned with the Bicycle Purge.

'It'll be buttons next, you mark my words,' the Widow Makepeace announced as she applied a poultice to the enormous egg on Moray's noggin. 'They'll collect 'em all up in big wagons and burn 'em … and then wonder why everyone's trousers keep fallin' down!'

She whooped with laughter at this one, banging the flat of her hand on the table and making various bowls spin about.

A grateful Moray held the healing poultice in place as the Widow busied herself fetching the tea things. He watched her small stooped figure hobble across the ramshackle shanty to a pile of debris, wherein she proceeded to rummage with the celerity of a spastic truffle pig.

The Widow Makepeace must have been at least a hundred years old. Her skin was shriven and stretched tight over her cheekbones. One eye was clouded and useless, while the other was a brilliant yellow with a rectangular pupil. Carbuncles jostled with moles for prominence on her chin, and the wattles on her neck hung like marzipan from the frame of a street seller's cart. She was dressed entirely in animal pelts, with tassels of mouse paws fringing the hem of her skirt. Her head had no hair to speak of, but for the stumpy, tough strands sprouting from the rinds of her ears. Covering her bald pate was a tall black conical hat with a wide brim that rather gave the game away, witch-wise.

Age had not done this to the Widow Makepeace. She had looked just as witchy when she'd come across Robert Moray drowning in a pond almost thirty years before. The boy had been skylarking on the slippery banks and fallen in. Just as he was going under for the last time, she'd plucked him from the water with her bony hand. They had been friends ever since and she had taught the doctor much in the way of magic. Of course, such things were behind him now.

'But you always liked the crystal ball,' complained the old woman.

The Widow knelt at the foot of an old camphor chest and extracted a large opaque orb. It was probably made of glass rather than crystal but was no less impressive for it. She held it reverentially in a square of red velvet, but Moray wanted no part of it. The weird rectangular yellow eye of the Widow Makepeace made an attempt at a puppy-dog appeal.

'Oh, all right,' relented Moray after an irritating minute of this. 'Once more, for old time's sake.' His head had stopped throbbing and he felt charitable.

When he was a young man, Moray had enjoyed gazing into the crystal ball with the old lady. Its whirling myriad hues had delighted him, as had her bold but fanciful foretelling of future events. It had all seemed so convincing back then.

Widow Makepeace screwed a pipe into her face and glided from the room as if on coasters. There was a clatter of wood, the thudding of metal and the shattering of crockery, whereupon she returned, cradling in her arms what a passing stranger might have taken for a translucent ostrich egg.

Moray was confused. 'But I thought you'd already taken the crystal ball out of the chest.' He turned to the box but it was closed.

Was it, perhaps, déjà vu?

The witch gave him a mysterious crooked smile. 'A mere lapse in continuity, my dear,' she laughed. 'Nothing a keen-eyed editor won't pick up before we go to print.'

A puzzled Moray paused a moment and then pushed away his teacup. He'd had enough of whatever hallucinogens it contained.

The Widow plonked the ball in the middle of the table and began running her kindling hands over it. Her eyelids fluttered and her voice became a fluting drone. Sparks stirred inside the glass sphere and shifting blue clouds swirled about as dark shapes emerged, pressing the imagination to make sense of them.

A tree. Black and dead and empty but for one leaf.

A magnificent white horse trots up. On its back sits King Charles I. (He has no head but Moray recognises him from the crown he's wearing on his neck.)

With a mighty swipe of the King's sword the tree is cleft in twain, and as the branches crash to the ground, the leaf flutters away.

Suddenly King Charles' head grows back, reinflating like a balloon. It grows to an enormous size and then explodes. Confetti and stardust rain down from the skies.

Slightly less suddenly, everything goes mauve and Doctor Moray awakens in a ditch. The hut is no more and Widow Makepeace is nowhere to be seen.

Chapter 7

**IN WHICH DOCTOR MORAY'S FRIEND
CHANGES HUMAN HISTORY**

*23rd day of October Anno Domini Iesu Christi 1657,
night, Godmanchester, East Anglia*

N THE SLOW TRIP HOME, MORAY mused on the meaning of his dream within a dream. King Charles was dead, but his son had survived and was living somewhere in Scotland. Could the Stuarts be planning to regain the Throne? Did the ailing tree represent Cromwell's line? Was the last remaining leaf Richard? Did the rain signify nothing more complicated than a *reign*? And why confetti and stardust and not something easier to clean up, like rice? All these questions Moray pondered as he pedalled.

An owl watched him as he sped past. Its head seemed to turn a full 360 degrees, but in reality it was only about 320. Still, it looked impressive.

A nearby vole, watching from a crack in a rock, spat out the cocoa he was drinking in surprise and scampered into his burrow.

Doctor Moray arrived home safely at 2 am, only to find a gnomish Dutchman in his kitchen, fiddling about with a microscope. Antony van Leeuwenhoek looked up from the eyepiece, startled, as Moray slammed the door and threw a bag of leeches down on the kitchen table.

'What the hell are you doing here?' demanded Moray as he drew the curtains. 'I've told you before I want nothing more to do with you, your microscopes, or your sick … frolics.'

Leeuwenhoek giggled and waved him over. 'Haff a loog at dis.'

Moray was wary; they had been through all this before. The Dutchman stood and backed away from the table, his arms raised in mock surrender. Only when he came to rest with a bump at the far wall, did Moray remove his bike clips and slide into the chair.

He fixed his orbital socket over the microscope's still-warm eyepiece and took in the magnified movements wriggling on the

The hunchbacked lens grinder from Delft

slide below. It was unlike anything Moray had ever seen. 'What is it? A tick?'

The hunchbacked lens grinder from Delft sauntered over to the table with a smugness that made you want to reach into the book and slap him.

'Well?' said Moray.

The tang of Leeuwenhoek's foul breath all but overwhelmed Moray as the microscopy expert bent down to whisper into the doctor's ear. 'Hit's nod a protist, nor eben a nematode. Nod eben a rotifer.'

Moray stifled his revulsion in the name of science. 'Well, what then?'

Drool spilled onto Moray's shoulder. ''Tis a … yooman cell.'

'By *yooman*, do you mean *human*?'

'Yah,' said Leeuwenhoek, a little shame-faced.

Leeuwenhoek had always been embarrassed about coming from Holland. And it wasn't just the ridiculous accent. He had always felt that Holland didn't actually qualify as a real country. Given that most of it was below sea level, it was really just an ocean. Sticking a big wall around it to keep the water out was living in denial. For a country to be a country, surely some visible surface area *above* the water was required. It was the same with Venice. That wasn't a city – it was a lake.

Leeuwenhoek had explained all this to Philip II of Spain while attempting to talk him out of signing the Treaty of Vervins, but Philip wouldn't listen and had chased him out of the palace with a broom. In the end, Leeuwenhoek had given up and tried to convince people he was French. This proved impossible. Not only could he not speak the language, but he couldn't even do a passable accent. He also refused to change his name, or wear anything other than wooden clogs; plus, he lived in a windmill in Amsterdam. Yeah, a nude, gay, smelly hunchback in clogs living in a windmill, whacked out on opium and making microscopes. How Dutch can you get?

This was why Leeuwenhoek sought out the company of men like Moray. Not only did they represent the strata of society to which he aspired, but they also provided a passport out of the marginalised undersea world into which he'd been born. The two men of science had met at a Lens-Grinding Weekend in Antwerp, drunk too much absinthe and woken in each other's arms the next morning, going over the Cascades de Coo in a barrel. On such flinty soil a mighty oak had sprung, and they had remained stout friends ever since.

&

TWO MONTHS ON FROM LEEUWENHOEK'S discovery, and Moray had managed to clone a Brazilian fire ant. He had just begun to experiment on the cellular material found in the late Richard Cromwell's leeches when he was arrested by the Witchfinder-General for his illicit bicycle rides. Someone had ratted him out. In exchange for his freedom, Moray agreed to name names. Thanks to his testimony, the Widow Makepeace was arrested and drowned. Moray also agreed to help the authorities with their ongoing investigation of Leeuwenhoek, who had long been suspected of occultist naughtiness.

Moray wore a parrot hidden under his vest during all his subsequent meetings with the Dutch émigré, and every conversation recorded by the parrot was later transcribed. It was an arduous process. The parrot had a learning difficulty and Moray would often have to trick Leeuwenhoek into repeating entire conversations, sometimes fifteen or twenty times. Eventually, enough evidence was amassed to establish a *prima facie* case.

Both the parrot and Doctor Moray gave evidence before the Witchfinder-General, Matthew Hopkins. The parrot later shot himself out of guilt. Moray's conscience was untroubled, though, and while Leeuwenhoek was taken in leg irons and chains to be tortured and tried, the Scot with friends in high places went on a cycling tour of Invisible Colleges throughout Britain.[8]

---

8. These colleges were not literally invisible, and were, in fact, made of regular building materials capable of being detected by the naked eye. The expression 'Invisible Colleges' refers to various groups of like-minded scientists who would gather in secret in these otherwise common-or-garden (and perfectly visible) buildings. It is not known what happened at these meetings, although apparently a lot of drinking went on and a bit of apron wearing. There is some talk in the minutes of a *Cloak* of Invisibility being owned by the Curator of Magnetics, William Ball; however, these reports are unconfirmed because Ball never used to hang it up and so could never find it.

Chapter 8

IN WHICH FUN IS HAD AT
MATTHEW REILLY'S EXPENSE

13th day of September Anno Domini Iesu Christi 2005,
09:32:37 ante meridiem GMT, Île de la Cité, Paris

 s I checked out of the Hotel Malte, François sidled up to me.

'Thank you for staying with us, monsieur,' he said, shaking my hand.

I thanked him back and watched him leave, then opened my hand to find a small nugget of paper. Unscrewed, it read:

> *Si vous cherchez la vérité*
> *derrière le breuvage magique*
> *de temps. 01.29.34.82.92.*
> *Jean-Noël Jeanneney*

If there is one thing I had in common with Leeuwenhoek, it was my inability to speak French. I showed the note to the concierge.

'If you seek the truth about the time potion,' he translated helpfully, 'ring Jean-Noël Jeanneney.'

'And the number?'

'I believe it is the *telephone* number, monsieur.'

'Yes, I understand that – but is it familiar to you?'

He regarded me sleepily. 'It is the Bibliothèque nationale de France, monsieur – on the rue de Richelieu.'

'May I use your phone?' My own lay charred somewhere in the no-doubt still-smouldering ruins of the Ossuary of Denfert-Rochereau.

'*Non*,' replied the concierge, turning away and pretending to sort through the mail. I could tell he was pretending because he didn't have any envelopes; he was just moving his hands quickly back and forth near the empty mail slots and humming. And yes, I was annoyed.

The concierge turned and looked at a point on the ceiling as if reading my thoughts which had somehow been projected there. 'The house phone is only for the use of *guests*, monsieur.'

'But I am a guest. I just checked out—' I protested.

'*Oui, c'est exact* – you just checked *out*, monsieur,' he snapped, and returned to his pantomimed mail sorting.

I gazed at the back of his head for a moment or two. When he started to hum the 'Hymne des Marseillais', I responded by la-la-la-ing 'Ça Plane Pour Moi'. I could see the hackles rise on the back of his neck, and I felt I'd made my point.

'Plastic Bertrand was Belgian!'[9] he shrieked, as I disappeared through the rotating doors and into a waiting taxi.

Tourists: 1. France: 0.

As I wasn't due at Charles De Gaulle Airport for another couple of hours, I decided to drop by the Bibliothèque and visit this Jean-Noël Jeanneney.

Jean-Noël turned out to be none other than the President of the Bibliothèque. A fussy little

---

9. *Yes, but using your logic, being Belgian and French are the same thing. Ed.*
Get fucked. Auth.

man with a bald head, horn-rimmed spectacles
and a luxuriant black moustache, he greeted me
warmly upon entering his office and offered me
a seat, but turned a little frosty when I told him
I was a writer seeking answers to a mystery. He
didn't trust writers of that type, he said. I asked
him why.

'Matthew Reilly,' he sniffed. 'He came
in here researching that – thing of his, you
know—' He interrupted his own sentence
with a dismissive wave of the hand.

'*Seven Ancient Wonders*?'

'No, no ... er—'

'*The Six Sacred Stones*?'

'No, no – oh, you know the one. What is
it?' Jean-Noël was clicking his fingers at me to
spur my memory.

'*The Five Greatest Warriors*?'

'No, no.'

'*Area 7*? *Ice Station*?'

'No.' He clicked some more.

'*Hell Island*?'

'No.'

'That online *Hover Racer* thing?'

Jean-Noël snorted derisively and gave up.
'Whatever it was it was dreadful; full of clichés

and riddled with hackneyed synonyms—'

'*Contest!*' I suddenly remembered.

Jean-Noël nodded sadly. 'Yes, that's the one.' He threaded his hands together. 'He wanted special access to our Rare Acquisitions Room ...'

He paused a moment, rose from his chair and walked to the window, hands now behind his back, his two fists knocking together. When next he spoke, it was in a voice overcome with emotion.

'He was only in there an hour with our Guttenberg Bible ... and when the guard came in—'

Jean-Noël's voice broke off as he choked on his words. I fetched him a small paper cone of water from the cooler, and when he had regained his composure he smiled at me with some embarrassment. Clutching the back of his antique Madison swivel chair, he continued.

'*He had eaten his sandwiches over it!*' Jean-Noël hissed in a whisper. The little man draped the back of his hand over his forehead in a gesture of disbelief worthy of Barrymore. 'Leviticus *was covered in crumbs!*'

'I can assure you, Mr President, that I would never think of doing such a thing.'

'And there was a coffee ring ...'

I shook my head sympathetically, at a loss for words.

'We had him beaten, of course.'

I cocked an incredulous eyebrow (mine). The President smiled knowingly and gave his chair an impressive spin; he was a man back in control.

'Oh yes, Charles Aznavour and his friends were more than happy to impress upon Monsieur Reilly what happens when one commits an infraction of the rules at the Bibliothèque nationale de France.'

'Charles Aznavour the singer?'

Jean-Noël spun his chair again and when it came to a stop, he shrugged gallically. 'Is there any other?'

'He must be eighty years old.'

Jean-Noël was spinning his chair around and around now. As it rose higher and higher, and eventually unscrewed itself from its base, we both watched in silence as it clattered to the floor.

'He is eighty-*one*,' said Jean-Noël with

a sniff. 'But he can swing a wheel brace at a man's knees with unerring accuracy.'

'I had no idea.'

'Why do you think he was awarded the Légion d'honneur in 1997?'

It was my turn to shrug.

'It certainly wasn't because of his singing,' scoffed Jean-Noël. 'Sometimes Sacha Distel accompanies him. They are quite a team – wonderful to watch; Distel holds the transgressor from behind and Aznavour punches them repeatedly in the stomach until they apologise. I don't approve of their methods but one cannot argue with the results. We have only been sued successfully once – by P. D. James. Aznavour's torching of her house was, shall we say, a little too enthusiastic.'

'Matthew is only young. I hope they went easy on him.'

'Killed by a car bomb,' announced Jean-Noël matter-of-factly.

'Gosh.'

'I quite agree. Personally, I abhor violence. Such measures were unheard of twenty years ago. If you had told me it would take Charles Aznavour, Sasha Distel and fifteen kilos of

C-4 to bring home to people the need to treat library books with respect, I would have sent you away with a flea in your ear. I don't know what has happened to the old values.'

God, this man was boring.

'Oh yes – I know what you are thinking. Surely not all our modern authors are so cavalier in their disregard for the etiquette of the Bibliothèque nationale de France? And, of course, you are right.' Jean-Noël peered at me over his horn-rims. 'Dan Brown – now there was a gentleman. Six weeks he spent in here copying out *The Holy Blood and the Holy Grail* and not so much as a crease in a page. A beautiful man, such lustrous hair and haunting aquamarine eyes ...' He gestured to the fireplace, over which hung a large framed photograph of the billionaire *Da Vinci Code* author, signed personally to Jean-Noël. 'Look at that chin – it is the chin of a genius.' He ran his finger down the cleft of his own and mourned its inadequacy. 'Mind you, I thought *Digital Fortress* was a piece of shit.'

I nodded dumbly and Jean-Noël changed the subject with a raise of his eyebrows. 'But

'Look at that chin – it is the chin of a genius.'

you are a friend of Alain Bauer, yes?'

Alain Bauer was a renowned French criminologist, constitutional lawyer and Freemason (Grand Master of the Grand Orient de France, in fact). He was the youngest ever Vice-President of the Sorbonne and for two years acted as the Chief Advisor on national security to President Michel Rocard. I had never heard of him.

'Yes, of course,' I improvised. 'I'm a great friend of Adam—'

'Alain,' corrected Jean-Noël, with a raise of his forefinger.

'Yes, yes, Alain. We're very good pals. We often go … snorkelling together.'

Jean-Noël knitted his brow. 'But I thought Alain suffered from aquaphobia.'

'Ah yes, did I say snorkelling? I meant … um – falconing.' (I thought I'd covered my gaffe beautifully.)

'Falconing?'

'Oh yes – if there's one thing my dear old chum, Adam—'

'Alain.'

'Yes … him as well. We all enjoy – the three of us – having … a large predatory bird perched on our wrist … you know, with the little mask on …' I blathered, patting Jean-Noël on the chest and arm in the manner of Bob Hope at his most cowardly. At one point I may have even referred to a suit of armour standing in the corner of the room as 'Laughing Boy'.

'And, you know,' I continued, drawing feeble pictures in the air with my fluttering fingers, the flop-sweat forming a pool around my shoes, 'you pull off the mask and it flies away – into the mountains ... and kills a mouse. Yes, truly the sport of kings.'

✑

WELL, I'LL SAY ONE THING FOR THE Bibliothèque nationale de France: nepotism opens doors, specifically the one to the Rare Acquisitions Room. Inside, on the huge redwood reading table, were the private diaries of Matthew Hopkins, Witchfinder-General of Cromwell's England. Included in the papers was the transcript of Antony van Leeuwenhoek's witch trial in 1689:

WITCHFINDER-GENERAL: *... and Mr Leeuwenhoek, what happened immediately after you showed Doctor Moray this 'yooman' cell?*

LEEUWENHOEK: *Nodding at all. We disguzt de scientific ramifikations, had a couble of bowlz of mead and den vent to bed.*

WITCHFINDER-GENERAL: *Nothing else?*

LEEUWENHOEK: *Vell ... I can't zee how my zex life could pozzibly be of interest to de Court——*

JUDGE: *Au contraire — I LOVE gossip!*

[Consternation! The Court is cleared and reconvenes the next day with a new Judge.]

NEW JUDGE: *Please proceed.*

WITCHFINDER-GENERAL: *Thank you, M'lud. Now, Mr Leeuwenhoek, a neighbour, Mrs Ethel Crabbe, says she saw you fly away from Doctor Moray's house on a broom. Is this true?*

LEEUWENHOEK: *Nonzense. I don't eeben own a broom.*

MRS CRABBE: *It could have been a rake!*

[Laughter]

NEW JUDGE: *Silence! I will not have unseemly behaviour in my Court. I don't know or care about what atmosphere my Brother Judge cultivated in here but I insist on decorum and will accept nothing less. The sanctity of this Chamber must be respected.* [farts] *Oh, Mother …*

WITCHFINDER-GENERAL: *What was that, M'Lud?*

NEW JUDGE: *Erm … nothing. Open a window please, Bailiff. Please proceed, Mr Witchfinder-General.*

WITCHFINDER-GENERAL: *Thank you, M'Lud. Now, Mr Leeuwenhoek, did anything unnatural go on in Doctor Moray's house that night?*

LEEUWENHOEK: *If de love of one man for anozzer in exchange for a high-powered microscope iz unnatural — den yah, something unnatural vent on.* [Pandemonium! The Court is cleared and reconvened the next day with an even newer Judge.]

EVEN NEWER JUDGE: *Please proceed.*
[Alarums! Again the Court is cleared but then reconvened when it is realised that everyone overreacted to what was a perfectly normal direction from His Honour.]

WITCHFINDER-GENERAL: *Thank you, M'Lud. Now, Mr Leeuwenhoek, the neighbour Mrs Crabbe also says that on the night in question you cast a magical spell and turned her husband into a horse.*

LEEUWENHOEK: *Dat'z ridoculous.*

WITCHFINDER-GENERAL: *Is it?* [Turning dramatically to the body of the Court] *Mr Crabbe, would you please stand up?*
[A horse stands.]

WITCHFINDER-GENERAL: *Are you Mr Lionel Crabbe of 53 Battington Crescent, Manningtree?*

HORSE: *I am.*
[Murmurs]

LEEUWENHOEK'S BARRISTER: *I object, M'lud. That horse is not under oath.*
[Again the Court is cleared [the even newer Judge escaping on Mr Crabbe] and reconvenes with a yet even newer Judge presiding.]

YET EVEN NEWER JUDGE: *All right, let's get down to cases. Mr Leeuwenhoek, the question is — are you or are you not a witch?*

WITCHFINDER-GENERAL: *Your Honour, that's …
sort of my job——*

YET EVEN NEWER JUDGE: *Shut up, you. Now, Mr
Leeuwenhoek?*

LEEUWENHOEK: *Yah, M'Lud. It's very zimple.
I showed Doctor Moray a yooman cell under my
microscope. He got de idea dat blood from Richard
Cromwell'z leeches cood be used to grow an
exakt replica of the same yooman being, much in
the way that a cutting of ivy can be used to grow
anodder whole new plant. We called diz notional
replicant yooman a clone, which iz de Greek word
for twig.*[10] *Over de enzuing monthz we had zome
zuccess with twig versionz of Brazilian fire antz
[Wasmannia auropunctata] but after rebeatedly
trying and failing to create a fully funktional twig
of Richard Cromwell ve realised dat science had a
plenty long way to go before it cood serve diz idea in
any praktikal zense. Zo, using a zpecial formoola
of rare snake's venom, ve, in de den Invisible
College, arranged to have Doctor Moray put in a
ztate of zuzpended animation and ztored in a
zecret lokation [togedder vith plentiful suppliez*

---

10. See, I told you.

of Richard Cromwell'z frossen blood for future experimendation] in de belief dat Doctor Moray cood be revived ven science kaught op vith him and he would den, bazically, create a yooman being parthenogenically and den sort of zend it back in time somehow to replaze de already dead son of our Lord Protector. And if dat'z witchkraft, I'll be a monkey's Oncle.

[Antony Van Leeuwenhoek was burned as a witch that afternoon.]

Chapter 9

IN WHICH POWER GOES TO OLIVER CROMWELL'S ROUNDHEAD

❧

15th day of January Anno Domini Iesu Christi 1658,
breakfast time, Huntingdon, East Anglia

ICHARD CROMWELL WAS ALIVE and well, and Alexander Pruitt had never felt more at home – which was odd, given that Alexander was inhabiting Richard's body.

He awoke each day with a new sense of purpose. He had a beautiful wife and three children, a father who loved him, servants, a jester, a few horses and a hundred acres of land. The last three months had made the Present seem a long, long time ago. His wounds had almost healed, and he was up and about most mornings, occasionally taking a stroll around the town. Yesterday, he had even bought a bun.

Doctor Moray recommended plenty of rest and it was on one of these occasions, while recumbent on his bed, mouth open and tongue fully extended for the doctor's approbation, that he learned something about his manifest destiny, which had he known anything about history he should have already known.

'You know your father expects you to take over the Lord Protectorship, now that your health has returned,' said Moray.

Alexander retracted his tongue. 'Really?' His mouth was dry and he reached for a goblet of water. A servant was at his side in an instant.

Moray was putting away his magnifying glass and leeches. 'So, do you think you're ready?'

Alexander thought for a moment. 'What is it my father does, exactly?'

Moray looked concerned. His patient was not completely back to normal. Occasionally he would talk in his sleep; rambling nonsense about fathers and foxes and grapes and murder. Moray's aide had jotted it all down in a journal but neither of them had been able to make head or tail of it. The doctor felt Alexander's brow and, detecting no fever, he shrugged and closed his satchel.

'I mean, I know he's the Lord Protector and all that, but what is it he actually *does*?'

'Follow me,' urged the desiccated Scot.

In a single audacious paragraph break they were gone, down a stone staircase to a fetid dungeon.

Moray paused briefly by a worn door. 'What ye are about t'see,' intoned the doctor in an unusually thick accent, 'may unfix ye wig and make ye unwelcome juice of sphincter greet thy pantaloons.'

And with that, the door cracked open.

Reclining on a swirl of silk was the nude form of the 77-year-old Lord Protector, his face upturned to his major-domo, who was busy tweezering off some of the old man's lesser moles. The arcing spurts of blood and wild flailing of arms made an interesting first impression.

'Ah, hello, son,' said the Lord Protector, finally looking over and staunching the flow of vermilion with a sponge the size of a sombrero. With his stray hand he motioned to a tasselled Turkish cushion, upon which Alexander dutifully sat. 'Doctor Moray tells me you are recovered.'

'I am feeling much better, Father,' admitted Alexander.

The Lord Protector gathered up his bolt of silk and wrapped it loosely about him as his major-domo backed away into the shadows to fetch a solid-silver biretta encrusted with sapphires. Cromwell slapped it to the floor and ground it under his heel.

The old man walked the full length of the hall across a carpet of rose petals to a massive oak coronation chair. A Nubian slave dusted the throne with his own beard just as Cromwell's arse was laid daintily upon it (the chair, not the beard), and a flurry of servants and axolotls[11] buzzed about and then disappeared, leaving the Lord Protector in an arresting tableau. On his head was perched Llewellyn's coronet, a most handsome golden crown ringed with ermine and surmounted by a bejewelled cross pattée into which was set 444 stones of inestimable worth. In his right hand he held a glittering sceptre made of gold

---

11. *Don't you mean acolytes? Axolotls are Mexican walking fish. Ed.*
No. I mean Mexican walking fish. Auth.

and peppered with rubies; in his left, a gold eagle-shaped ampulla containing a mystical oil that could only be extracted by midgets from the pineal gland of a sperm whale during a full moon, which he was even now in the process of pouring into a diamond-flecked pearl-handled Anointing Spoon held at right-angles between the brilliantly white and symmetrically perfect teeth of a crouching virgin negress swathed entirely in gold silk samite.

'I am not one for the trappings of office,' Cromwell announced wearily to his son. 'It is time you took over as Lord Protector.'

'Really? Can you do that?' asked Alexander. 'Shouldn't I get voted in or something?'

'Vote?' Cromwell smiled to himself. Then he smiled to Alexander. There wasn't much difference between the two smiles, and it may well be that he was smiling both to himself and Alexander each time or that it was simply one long smile with no break. Or it could be that he didn't smile to himself at all and that maybe he just overheard his smile to Alexander. In any event – he smiled; that's the important point.

'My people are too ignorant to vote,' he continued, sensibly ignoring any confusion. 'They need someone to look out for their interests in these perilous times ... and that someone is ME!!!!'

I do not use capitals or exclamation marks lightly. Cromwell really yelled that last word. The negress crouching at his feet got such a surprise that she bit the handle of the Anointing Spoon in two. Cromwell, whose mercy had been tempered during the strain of the last few months, had her put to death. That night he dined on her roasted carcass.

'More skull?' he offered his son.

'No, no ...'

'You disapprove?' asked Cromwell, sensing his son's disapproval.

'Well, cannibalism ...' Alexander left the word hanging, feeling that was enough.

'What of it?'

'Well, it just seems ...' and here Alexander cleared his throat. 'It's just that I'm not sure cannibalism fits in with the underlying principles of Puritanism.'

This gave Cromwell pause. He placed the fracture of cranial bone back on his plate. 'I'm sure brain-eating is allowed ...' he pondered.

'I don't think so, Father.'

Cromwell clapped his hands magisterially and his servants melted away. He dabbed the corners of his mouth with a solid-gold napkin and pushed back from the table. 'I have become as bad as King Charles,' he announced glumly. 'Decadent. Imperious. Arrogant.'

Alexander was reasonably sure that the vices of the recently abridged Charles I did not include the eating of human flesh and internal organs but wisely kept his own counsel.

'That ...' continued the Lord Protector, '... is why I must name you as my heir. You shall be Lord Richard Cromwell the First, Protector of the Commonwealth of England, Ireland and Wales.'

'... and Scotland, your Majesty,' whispered Cromwell's major-domo, as diplomatically as he could from a nearby cupboard.

'Ah yes,' nodded the current Lord Protector, closing his eyes. 'Scotland. Of course.'

Cromwell didn't like being corrected. Not in public, not in private, and certainly not from a cupboard. He rose, drew his Great Sword of State, walked over to the cupboard

He tripped over a step and fell out of a casement window.

and ran it through several times. Each time the blade splintered through the wood, a muted squawk could be heard from within. Then nothing.

Cromwell wiped the sword on the Nubian's beard and slid it back into his scabbard. 'Yes, how could I forget dear old Scotland. Thank you, major-domo … Remind me to give you a posthumous honour of some kind.' There was no reply. Cromwell bristled. 'Have his body thrown into the Tiber. If there's one thing I can't abide, it's dumb insolence.'

A guard nodded, bowed and backed out of the room as best he could, knocking over tables and upending a few decorative suits of armour. The poor man wasn't sufficiently familiar with the layout of the Great Room to walk backwards with any confidence, but dared not turn around lest he incur the wrath of his ruler. Eventually he tripped over a step and fell out of a casement window, into the moat several stories below, whereupon he was promptly eaten by crocodiles. The Lord Protector gave Alexander a long-suffering look.

'Isn't the Tiber in Italy?' mused another guard in a moment of ill-advised audibility.

'What?' queried Cromwell through clenched teeth.

'The River Tiber. It's in Rome, isn't it? My sister went there last year for a holiday—'

'I *know* where it is,' lied the Lord Protector. 'I want the body in the cupboard shipped there immediately and thrown into it. That *is my edict*.'

The guard screwed up his face a little. 'Gee, that's gonna take some time to organise. You know, I think we'd have to fill in a few forms … What about Avignon? I hear the anti-Pope's a real pushover—'

Cromwell was very nearly bursting with anger.

'I WANT HIS BODY DUMPED IN THE TIBER!!!!!! IS THAT UNDERSTOOD???!!!!!!!'

'Yeah, yeah, yeah …' answered the guard quickly. 'It's just that getting a body – particularly a murder victim – on a boat, through customs, past the Port Authority in Rome; then there's council permission – I mean, it's probably *illegal* to dump a body in the river just like that … 'cos my sister had enough trouble getting her kid into the Vatican … Mind you, it did have leprosy—'

'See to it,' hissed Cromwell in a final sinister whisper.

'Excuse me?' said the guard.

Cromwell stared at him for a few seconds, drumming his fingers on the side of the blood-drenched cupboard, then looked to Alexander, who was eating an apple. Alexander shrugged.

The guard continued, oblivious to the Lord Protector's sky-rocketing intra-cranial pressure. 'Sorry, I couldn't hear you, my Liege. You were speaking a bit soft there.' He grinned.

A fatal error.

Cromwell turned with the menace of a slavering dog stalking a slightly retarded badger. His voice bubbled just a few tantalising degrees from complete lack of control. 'Just see to it – and while you're there, do make sure to throw your own body in the Tiber as well – after first making sure to behead yourself.'

A thin smile played on Cromwell's reedy lips. The guard smiled back with a goofiness reminiscent of Keanu Reeves in the *Bill and Ted* movies, a moment of anachronistic charm quite understandably lost on the Lord Protector.

Then the guard stopped smiling and furrowed his temple in a dim thought. 'You know,' he mused, 'I'm not sure I can cut off my own head – and *then* throw myself in the Tiber.'

'TRY IT THE OTHER WAY AROUND THEN!!!!' bellowed the old man.

'Okey-dokey,' said the guard as he attempted to drag the cupboard from the room.

Oliver Cromwell looked to his son for comfort and understanding, but Alexander Pruitt had already escaped through a priest's hole.[12]

---

12. Priest's holes were a very popular feature in homes of the 1600s and were invented by Nicholas Owen as a means of hiding Catholic priests – who were very embarrassing – during the reign of Elizabeth I. Owen won many awards and was eventually canonised for his Services to Interior Design. 'His use of light and limited space was a revelation,' wrote his executioner, Richard Topcliffe, in *Ladies Home Companion*. 'In his final hours he worked miracles in our dungeon with nothing but a couple of throw cushions and a leopard-print rug.'

Chapter 10

∽

*13th day of September Anno Domini Iesu Christi 2005,
20:32:37 post meridiem GMT, Paris, France*

HE SEATBELT SIGN PINGED OFF
and as the outskirts of Paris slipped
under the clouds, I kicked off my
shoes to do those clenching exercises that are
supposed to prevent thrombosis.

I was out of the woods – or, at least, partly.
Stowed away in the cargo hold of the plane
was Alexander Pruitt's coffin; my manuscript
thus far had been posted off to my agent for
safekeeping; and Charlie, who had met me at
Charles De Gaulle,[13] and I were on our way
to America to meet with someone who was
going to bring the old man's boy back to life.

---

13. The airport, not the dead French President.

The note secreted in the base of the stone sepulchre in the Midlothian crypt had named this man, but had done so using German ciphers from the World War II Enigma machine and so we'd had to break into the Imperial War Museum and enlist the aid of Colossus Mk II to decode it. The nightwatchman who helped us plug it in was just as surprised as we were when his prized exhibit typed out the name Doug Henning.

By night, a harmless Las Vegas magician who worked a lot with scarves; by day, a sorcerer of unlimited diabolical power – it was even said that Henning was the one who'd brought Roy back to life after Siegfried's tiger had eaten him. Alexander may not have been torn apart and digested, but his revivification was still going to be quite a trick for the famous moustachioed rabbit-faced hippie.

৵

WHEN I LEFT THE FOX AND GRAPES ALL those months ago, I had nothing to go on. I put Una onto it and, as usual, she didn't let me down. She came up with the name of a low-level Mason she thought might be helpful: Alfie Gaff.

Gaff turned out to be very helpful indeed. Too helpful for his own good, perhaps. We were to have met again last night but events did not unfold in the pleasantly origamic fashion that either of us had anticipated – and this morning's *l'Humanité* reported that a body had been found in the blackened rubble of the Denfert-Rochereau. Poor old Gaff would no longer be of help to anyone.

Back when he was alive, though, it had been quite a different story. Alfie Gaff had been full of advice as we'd chugged our way up north. In fact, he never stopped talking once we left London. Or eating. The first-class railway carriage was very comfortable, but I spent most of the journey dodging flecks of pastry as my travelling companion spoke at me at length of the Rosicrucian Death Squads. At the time, I thought he was exaggerating.

'No, no, no – you gotta watch out for 'em,' said Gaff, leaning in so he couldn't miss me. 'Galileo started 'em up originally, after them heresy convictions. He got some of the bigger lads from his Lodge to pop around to Pope Paul V's.'

My nose was sprayed with spittle on each 'p'. I adjusted the angle of my head slightly.

'Oh, they made a right mess – paintin' socks on Michelangelo's *David*, re-sculptin' the nose of Mary in the *Pietà* so it was fifteen feet long, wallpaperin' over the Sistine Chapel frescoes …'

He had an Irish brogue – in fact, he wore two of them.

My nose was now at risk of being completely lost under Gaff's ad hoc *découpage*. I jerked out of range now and then, timing my movements with the rock and sway of the train so as not to appear rude. When Gaff wolfed down another cream cake, I took the opportunity to slip in a question about the large mysterious box that Doctor Moray had shipped to Scotland only a few days before.

'Ooh, yes, yes … 'tis very strange, that,' he whispered, narrowing his eyes. 'A large box, it was. I just took it to the station—'

'Large enough to hold a body, do you think?'

Gaff finished what he'd been eating, paused a moment and then picked up an éclair.

'Could be, yes,' he said, before popping it into his mouth whole. 'Mind you,' he continued, his voice a little muffled by the cream, 'I'm not saying the Doc killed nobody. All's I know is he were very keen for me not to tell no-one about it.'

Alfie Gaff intrigued me. He had an Irish brogue – in fact, he wore two of them – and mixed in there somewhere was a bit of Scots and West Country plus a hint of Welsh. It was an unusual hybrid that made him come across like a hillbilly version of Sean Connery doing an impression of Charo. His voice was the most normal thing about him.

Weighing in at 300 kilos and standing about 215 centimetres high in his stockinged feet, he was an imposing physical specimen. Your eye would have been easily caught at silly mid-on by his enormous red beard; long enough to not only obviate any need for a tie but also for shirt buttons and a belt buckle. Swathed as he was in every conceivable clan of tartan and sporting plastic fox masks over his knees, one could tell he was no slave to fashion. Plus, he was black – and I mean *really* black. That sort of deep, dark, almost purple black you get in the Masai. Also, his head was tiny; about a fifth the size of an average human head. The overall effect was like looking at a squash ball balanced on a giant kilted hot water service.

'Oh, to be sure,' continued Gaff, 'Doctor Moray is a good 'un. He saved me leg, he did.' For emphasis, he tapped his left leg below the knee with a praline.

'Yes, but your leg is wood, isn't it?' (There is nothing more unmistakable than the sound of chocolate on willow.)

Gaff gave a nod and popped the comestible into his mouth, pausing only briefly before swallowing it whole.

'But I don't understand. If your leg is made of wood, how did he—'

''Twas on fire,' he replied, impatiently. 'Old Doc Moray threw a bucket of sand on it.'

Having finished all the food (and, it seemed, the conversation), Gaff lit up a long-stemmed briar pipe.

'We was on a tanker ship bound for Zanzibar in '68,' he resumed (I was wrong about the conversation), looking wistfully out the corridor window at a passing dessert trolley as he puffed. 'The Doc could have thrown me overboard into the Channel, you know, but he dinnae want to wake me ... Ah, yes, I be indebted to that mon for the rest of me natural life.'

'But then ... why are you helping Charlie Pruitt?'

'Because,' he interrupted (a little too late, given I'd finished what I was saying), giving his other leg a tap with his pipe for emphasis, 'Charlie fought with me in Africa in '42. Saved this leg when it caught fire in El Alamein. Dragged me through a minefield, into the Nile. A mon doesn't forget that ...' His voice trailed off to nothing.

'Gee, that's pretty unlucky – your legs catching alight twice in your life like that,' I suggested, trying to jumpstart the conversation.

'Life's pretty unlucky,' he mused. 'Never again, though. I vowed that after France.'

'Yes ... though it did happen again, didn't it?'

'What?'

'The leg-catching-fire business.'

'Only once,' he conceded, tapping on his leg again, 'but it just stiffened me resolve that it would … never – happen – again.'

Tap. Tap. Tap.

Burning tobacco fell out of Gaff's pipe and onto his wooden leg with each tap. His knee started to smoulder a little and eventually a flame took hold. Such was the intensity of Gaff's reverie that it was a full minute before he noticed.

At first, I wasn't sure he hadn't intended it; he was, after all, a rather theatrical man. Eventually, his thrashing about convinced me that the conflagration in his lap was no mere affectation but a genuine emergency, and so I raced into the corridor and grabbed a fire extinguisher from the wall. By the time we arrived in Edinburgh's Waverley Station, Gaff was completely covered in foam and I had earned myself a comrade for life. Life, though, would turn out to be a lot shorter for one of us than either of us could ever have imagined.[14]

---

14. Sorry. A bit awkwardly expressed. I'm referring to the fact that he dies later on. *Supra*.

❧

LODGE ROSSLYN ST CLAIR NO. 606 IS A
Scottish Masonic Lodge situated in the county
of Midlothian, just outside Edinburgh.
Alfie Gaff and I took a hansom cab from
the station and arrived at Mrs Ambrose's
Bed 'n' Breakfast just after nightfall. Sadly,
the eponymous Mrs Ambrose was not there
to greet us, having already retired to her
bed with her husband, Bert. 'For a night of
unbridled passion,' explained the night porter
a little unnecessarily. Instead, her daughter
Caliope was there to lend a hand, carrying
our trunks on her back to the sixth floor while
we partook of a whisky in the lounge.

'Arrggh, she be a right looker,' observed
Gaff of Caliope's disappearing rump as she
clomped up the stairs. 'A lot like that lassie
o' yours, eh?' He gave me a cheeky smile and
then crammed a fistful of complimentary bar
snacks into his gob.

'Yes, yes – very attractive girl.' To be honest,
I hadn't noticed, having just come in from
paying the cabbie. From the back though, she
did look a lot like Una.

Gaff leaned into me, crunching. 'Milk-white skin – alabaster shoulders – neck like a porcelain doll's.'

'Well … not a lot of sun up this way, I expect,' I pondered, still thinking about Una.

'And did ye get a load of them gams?'

'Her what?'

He looked around. There were a couple of tweedy sorts over by the fireplace, playing draughts. His voice dropped to a whisper. 'Her gams, mon. Her pins …'

I looked at him blankly.

'Her fokkin' legs,' he guttered with exasperation. Slivers of nut and sultana peppered my cheek.

'Oh yes – they were indeed delightful. Both of them.'

The bartender splashed out another couple of neats. Gaff asked for the snack bowl to be refilled, and the man glowered at him with traditional Scottish hospitality before stomping back into the kitchen.

'Perhaps …' continued Gaff with a barely contained giggle – but then he just waggled his eyebrows.

'I'm sorry?'

'You know …' He waggled his eyebrows some more, as if this would clarify things, and then made a giddy-up noise with his tongue and teeth. 'You know … the lassie.'

I looked up at the empty landing.

Gaff winked at me insanely for a couple more seconds and then downed the remainder of his whisky. He then proceeded to unroll a document on the bar while rolling his eyes and muttering. It was a floor plan, and it told me all I needed to know about Lodge Rosslyn St Clair No. 606.

❧

UNDER THE COVER OF THE DARKNESS afforded us by night-time we made our way to the Lodge. Alfie Gaff had all the requisite keys but we still needed to climb over the enormous flagstone wall at the rear in order to get to the main building, a three-hundred-year-old stone cottage.

In this regard, Gaff's size was both a blessing and a curse. While I could stand on his shoulders and easily reach the top of the fence, then pull myself over, Gaff could not. If he stood on my shoulders, he'd kill me;

and standing on his own shoulders, while not impossible given he could remove his legs, would only get him halfway up. In the end, I had to go back into town and hire a small crane so I could winch him over the wall. That was the plan, anyway – unfortunately, Gaff had a fear of heights. Anything over twelve feet had him shrieking like Fay Wray. I should have remembered this.

When we'd tried a spot of train surfing on the trip from London, he hadn't made it even a quarter of the way up the caboose ladder before he was competing with the engineer's whistle for shrillness. I kicked him in the balls to shut him up but it only made things worse. Fortunately, he was beaned unconscious by the keystone in the entrance to the Welwyn Tunnel. He'd spent most of the trip from Digswell in a coma.

Mind you, it's all relative, isn't it? Screaming while hanging ten on a speeding locomotive turned out to be far less of a worry than being hoisted over a wall by a Farmi KV155 crane winch.

Startled by Gaff's banshee act, I accidentally knocked the gear lever with my knee and reversed through the wall, a wishing well and into an ornamental fountain. Gaff's head became lodged inside the bronze shell of the Geraardsbergen *Manneken Pis* (a replica), and he was only spared from drowning after I weltered away at the urinating infant with a claw hammer for the better part of an hour before finally cracking it open. It was a miracle no-one heard us.

Gaff must have had a hundred keys on the enormous ring he carried with him, and he must have used each and every one as we made our way from room to room, from corridor to corridor, through each and every secret door and sliding panel until, finally, we entered the chamber in the centre of the Lodge.

Inside were thousands of shelves full to groaning with thousands of leather-bound books, each containing thousands of ink-spattered pages of hand-written minutes, taken from countless Masonic meetings over the last few centuries. There were also thousands of dusty letters, notes and other jottings piled here and there, tied with green ribbon.

The documents were catalogued using a system devised in 1710 by an eight-year-old blind peasant girl from Reims. Unfortunately, the secret to the Lodge's cataloguing system died with her when she plummeted to her death from the highest turret of Monte Cassino, having been pushed by a murderous hook-handed abbot during an otherwise uneventful sightseeing holiday through the Italian Alps.

What captured our attention, however, were the two stone sarcophagi in the centre of the room. On each was an ornately carved figure of a gryphon, rampant on a bed of asphodel.

'Ah ha!' yelled Gaff triumphantly as, a few moments later, he edged the lid off one of the coffins, just enough to see the pale face of the young man inside. 'I believe ye owe me a fiver, mon.'

I looked up from the other casket, dumbfounded, having managed to lever the lid off with a tyre iron. Gaff's expression changed from smug to utter bewilderment. Inside my coffin lay the same pale-faced young man.

Chapter II

*23rd day of October Anno Domini Iesu Christi 1898,
05:31:11 ante meridiem GMT, Roslin Glen, Midlothian*

IDLOTHIAN IS A QUIET COUNTY. That was the whole idea, I guess. When Richard/Alexander's body was moved there from London in the late 1890s, it was important it be done without too much fuss. Fortunately for those involved, there were enough of the Brotherhood working at British Rail and in the Midlothian constabulary to ensure suspicions were not raised – at least, not to an investigative level – at the sight of a well-iced casket making its way on the back of a wagon along Edinburgh's Royal Mile in the dead of night, through Bungarrig Park and up a sinuous path to the rear of the Lodge, where a special chamber had been prepared in the mausoleum.

For the high-level Rosicrucian Masons party to this intrigue, the proceedings were unusual in their lack of ceremony. For them, the act of opening a door could take up to an hour and require several changes of clothing, but that night they acted with the expedite swiftocity of regular men with something to hide – and fear. The crypt was quickly sealed and, according to their ancient instructions, Charlie's son was to remain there undisturbed for a century – and he would have, had I not happened across him.[15]

Of course, despite the placement of the preceding two paragraphs, nothing could have been further from my mind as I relaxed, feet up and seat back, in a privately chartered midnight-blue Gulfstream 560 that plunged like a dirty fist through the twilit Pacific sky, on its way to a resounding sock on the glass jaw of LA and bang onto the canvas for a one-on-one count with the Mike Ovitz of Hollywood talent agency colossus MCG, Mike Ovitz.

---

15. Or is it 'them'? Not sure. (N.B. Check with editor about what makes more sense before book is published.)

My agent, Claude B, had sent some draft chapters of my book to various studio heads, and apparently the word on the Ventura Boulevard was that I had a sure-fire-green-lit-multi-million-dollar-go-project-hit on my hands. Ovitz had sent an urgent wire insisting I break off the very adventure I was living, and fly over to discuss terms. My agent met Charlie and me at LaGuardia. He was wearing an $8000 Armani suit.

'Don't worry, I can afford it,' he reassured us both. He put his arm around Charlie as if he'd known him all his life. 'With what they're gonna be paying us, I can wear four or five of these suits at once on a straight, no bullshit, 15 per cent cut.'

Charlie looked at me, worried. Five suits at once?

It sounded crazy. But Hollywood is a crazy town. Nonetheless, I recommended extreme caution. I'd heard about these Los Angeles movie-mogul sharks.

Claude laughed and clapped me on the back as we boarded our plane to LA, reassuring me that he knew exactly what he was doing. Hell, he'd once represented the guy who played

Catweazle, and while he'd died penniless and forgotten, he never had half the talent I had. He then proceeded to be thoroughly obnoxious throughout the trip: pinching the stewardesses, ordering the kosher meal to look more Jewish, and even inviting the only other passenger on board (Barbra Streisand) to join the Mile High Club. Eventually, he had to be sedated by the crew and strapped into his seat. He woke as we hit the west coast and managed to pull himself together a little as we made our approach.

'I'm cool, I'm cool,' he kept repeating, obviously still excited and leaning over Charlie to look out the window. 'Lookee there – it's the Brown Derby.'

He was looking at a reflection of the hat he was wearing. I swiped it from his head and hit him with it.

'Shouldn't we be meeting this magician fellow about Alexander?' asked Charlie, not unreasonably.

'It's on the way, it's on the way,' Claude assured the old man. Then, twisting his mouth in my direction and adopting a stage whisper that would embarrass even Simon Callow:

'You keep Grandad busy at the Holiday Inn while I take the meeting. We don't want to come across as rubes with a guy like Ovitz.'

Claude gave me a wink, smiled innocently at Charlie and then started reading the laminated Emergency Card. After a while he leaned in to confide to me: 'You know, this is the first time I've flown in a plane.'

'Maybe *I'd* better take the meeting—' I suggested.

'I'm cool, baby—'

'I don't think people call each other "baby" in Hollywood anymore.'

Claude tapped his nose and nodded. 'Yeah – sophisticated. I got you.' Then he indicated the in-flight headset around his neck. 'Do we get to keep these?'

I snatched the headset from him and emptied his pockets of several bags of peanuts. The stewardess looked over from the curtain.

'Maybe he should stay at the hotel and *I* should take the meeting?' suggested Charlie.

'As long as I get my 15 per cent,' agreed Claude.

When we touched down with much squealing of tyres, and even more squealing

Claude grabbed at her leg and
tried to look up her dress.

from Claude, an Air Marshall greeted us in the arrival lounge and shot him with a stun net. Barbra Streisand had to step over his semiconscious, slightly twitching body and, as she did so, Claude grabbed at her leg and tried to look up her dress. He was severely beaten by the burlier members of her waiting entourage. Charlie took him ahead to the Holiday Inn and I grabbed a cab to Beverly Hills.

∽

'TOM CRUISE IS VERY INTERESTED IN playing you,' said Mike Ovitz as he chopsticked a piece of raw salmon into his gob.

We were enjoying a working lunch in the agent's exclusive Sino-American–influenced office. Dishes were wheeled in and out and contracts were fluttered about courtesy of a bevy of unfeasibly attractive men and women, each proffering a Mont Blanc for Ovitz to sign with.

Around his office hung hundreds of framed photographs, mostly of the famous agent alongside his many, equally famous, A-list clients: Tom Cruise, Morgan Freeman, Tom Cruise, Meryl Streep, Robert De Niro, Tom Cruise, Scarlett Johansson, Al Pacino, Tom Cruise, Robert Redford, Tom Cruise (four consecutive pictures), Howie Mandel and, finally, another large picture of Tom Cruise. This one was different from the others in that it wasn't a conventional portrait; rather, it was a long shot of Cruise sitting alone in a waiting room, reading a magazine. A study in the solitude of celebrity, perhaps? No, it was a window – Tom Cruise was actually sitting in Ovitz's waiting room.

'Would you like to meet him?' asked Ovitz, rummaging around in his desk drawer.

'Sure,' I said. I'd been a fan ever since *Vanilla Sky*.

Ovitz produced a small whistle and blew into it. I didn't hear a thing but Cruise did. He looked up from his magazine, his smile breaking into an even bigger one when he saw Ovitz wave him in. With one bound he was at the door.

'Hey, how are you, buddy?' enthused Cruise as he pumped my hand, his beaming teeth an impossible white. 'Love the book ... it's got a real kinda WOW, you know?' I didn't, but smiled and nodded back as he paced the plush carpet, gesticulating in wild jabs, pointing at Ovitz and making pistol shots. He spun around at the window and whipped off his original Ray-Ban Wayfarer 2140s, flashing a pair of contact-lensed baby blues. 'Gotta do the film ... let's make it happen ... YEAH!!!' He let out a little yelp and assumed a karate pose, which he held for a full awkward minute before bursting into laughter and punching me on the arm. 'Man, it's – WOOOH! ... Let's – GO FOR IT!!!'

Hollywood. It *was* a crazy town – and I loved it.

Ovitz suggested we take in a Vegas show and Cruise leapt at the chance (literally), insisting he be our guide. Hoping to kill two birds with one stone, I suggested we make it Doug Henning. A frenzied cellular phone call later, tickets were arranged and we were piling into a stretch limo purring kerbside on Rodeo Drive, a liveried black man at the wheel. Ovitz begged off at the last minute, claiming he had to go to the toilet, but he assured me I was in good hands with his Number One client.

Tom Cruise was, and is, a fascinating creature. He's not a Mason but a Scientologist. He is said to be the Chosen One of a religion that is, essentially, about making rich people feel okay about themselves while being electrocuted through a tin can. I hadn't quite realised just how prominent a figure Cruise was in the organisation until I got in the limo and noticed L. Ron Hubbard sitting in the back seat.

'Gosh!' I gushed, sliding in. 'I thought L. Ron Hubbard was dead.'

'He is!' enthused Cruise. 'I had him stuffed and he rides with me for good luck.'

Cruise slammed the door, let out a whoop and we pulled into the blur of traffic.

'The Commodore travels with me everywhere,'

announced Cruise. 'He advises me … yeah!!!
GO FOR IT!!!'

The star cracked open the sunroof and,
laughing uproariously, began waving at the
street signs and telephone poles whizzing past
as we sped out of town on the Interstate.

Chapter 12

*15th day of January Anno Domini Iesu Christi 1658,
just after breakfast, Thetford Forest, East Anglia*

LEXANDER Pruitt ran through the forest, the branches scraping against Richard Cromwell's face as he did so. He didn't know where he was running to, but he knew he wanted to get back; back to his own body and his own Time. Not for the first time, he found he didn't belong anymore.

Soon enough he happened across the hunched form of Leeuwenhoek, bent over a lichen-covered log and peering at the progress of one of his newly cloned Brazilian fire ants. The Dutch lens grinder let out a yelp as the younger man tripped over him. Alexander was full of apologies.

'Zink notting ob it,' chuckled Leeuwenhoek, waving away the stranger's concern and grateful for some human contact.

'Pardon?'

The grotesque Delftian was taken with the politeness of the handsome stranger. No-one had been this kind to him since he'd been beaten and thrown off a bridge in Angkor by a Good Samaritan twelve years ago. Even Moray, his best friend, was openly hostile most of the time.

As Alexander dusted the dirt and leaves from Leeuwenhoek's cape, the blushing Hollander did a quick audit of his injuries. 'A grazz stein on mein jodhpurs, a graze on mein elboin ... a brogen toe ...'

Alexander picked up the older man's shattered bug-catcher. Most of the ants had escaped. In two hundred years, their descendants would wipe out all the badgers in Europe.

'Where waz yoo goink in zuch a hooray, eh?'

'What?'

'He wants to know why you were running through the forest, lad,' explained a helpful, and familiar, Scottish voice.

Doctor Moray stepped out from behind a tree. 'I hope you don't mind me following you,' he continued. 'I was taking my morning constitutional around the castle gardens when I saw you swimming across the moat.'

Alexander explained the whole mad story, not expecting either man to believe him. When he was done, Leeuwenhoek turned in amazement to Moray.

'Cood it be?' he whispered.

Moray stayed his confederate with a gesture. Their experiments with ants were one thing, but to have made a *twig* from human cells was unthinkable. Or was it? Leeuwenhoek's results had been encouraging. Maybe all they needed was time. But this business about Moray being alive more than three hundred years from now – how was such a thing possible?

❧

1947. A LIQUORICE FARMER IN PONTEFRACT was digging up an aniseed stump when he inadvertently unearthed several hundred small earthenware jars. Inside each one was a tiny scroll made of animal skin. So delicate were the scrolls that the first turned to dust when the

A liquorice farmer in Pontefract

farmer attempted to open it. This happened twice, then a third and fourth time ... Six hundred and seventy-three attempts later, the farmer gave up and sold the remaining five scrolls to a passing ostler, who promptly destroyed three of them by also attempting to open them (at the farmer's insistence).

Mercifully, the ostler donated the two remaining scrolls to the Qumran University, where they eventually found their way to the Ancient Languages Department and into the trembling hands of Professor Gillian

Blaylock-Stein, who promptly destroyed one of them when she tried to open it. When a translation of the sole surviving scroll was published in the *Biblical Archaeological Review*[16] three years later, it set the world of Theology on its ear, for it was nothing less than the first draft of a page from St Augustine's *Confessions*.

The discovery proved something hitherto unknown: that St Augustine did not, in fact, write his manuscripts – he dictated them to a secretary. The freewheeling sentence structure, the equivocations and the poor grammar all point to an *extempore* approach, probably the result of St Augustine's inability to hold a quill.[17]

The Blaylock-Stein Draft Page Scroll belongs to the fifth volume of the thirteen that make up the *Confessions*, and deals with St

---

16. Later reprinted in *Dolly* (Mar. 1989).
17. Due to repeated bee stings on his knuckles brought on by his insatiable lust for honey, his insistence on simply reaching into the hive with his bare hands and his phobia about apiarist gloves. *Ref. St Augustine: Fat Greedy Pig* by Archbishop George Pell (1972), Libreria Editrice Vaticana, p. 3289.

Augustine's early manhood in Numidia in the north of Africa – specifically, in the town of Tagaste, not far from Hippo, where he would eventually become Bishop.

In this extract, he and his four-year-old son, Adeodatus, are on a hymenoptera-gathering holiday in Souk-Ahras, when they come across a dead mule in a cave:

7 *And so it came to pass that we didst chance upon a cave and shelter from the rain. For, behold, we hadst this day collected several wasps and a plentiful supply of bees and so were verily about to give humble and most deserving thanks to thee, O Lord, for thy bounty whicheth underlieth all things. But my son, Adeodatus, from whose mother's loins he hadst begat, didst point out an animal lying beyond the mouth of the cave. And my eyes, O Lord, having not adjusted to the change in light, causeth me confusion as to the nature of the aforementioned animalculas. 'Is it another wasp, my dutiful son?' quoth I. 'No, Father, it is not,' bespoke my son. 'Then what?' I spake, still within the mire of puzzlement that I, betwixt knowing and unknowing, was. 'For, behold, I know it is a mule,' vouchsafed Adeodatus.*

8 And forsooth it was a mule – that unholy union betwixt horse and donkey, and it appeared, O Lord, to be dead and half eaten. But Lo – thy merciful hand, O Lord, had been stayed in the Choir Invisible joining department, for whilst the half-eaten sterile hybrid quadruped alluded to in my son's previous utterance did certainly appeareth dead – it was not. For when that which was born of his fleshly parents and one of those fleshly parents himself (me) did bringest home this mule for purposes scientific (I assure you), it didst move. But, O Lord, nor didst it move immediately upon its arrival as if it were asleep or something, but, O Lord, nigh on four months thereafter! Yea and verily so – imagine if you will, O Lord, how surprised we were. Very. Four Months! For our studies revealed thy mule, in Your great and infinite wisdom, had been bitten by a Gaboon Adder.

9 As you, O Lord, would no doubt be awarest, as your omnipresence and infinite knowledge is pretty comprehensive – the Gaboon Adder wilst often attackest and fang its prey, even if it be a hundred times bigger than itself, and wilst then dragst it back to its cave to consume over several months, but – and here's the beauty of the creature's *design, O Lord (which, again, thee would obviously be fully cognisant of) — the venom of the snake keeps the prey alive — but yet in an immobilised state — until it be fully eaten.*

10 *And it came to pass that the Gaboon Adder died of a heart attack part-way through its meal and the mule, despite being half eaten, awoke and ran away. Imagine, O Lord! — as I'm sure you can (given that if your imagination is equal to even half of your omnipotence, it'd be pretty vivid) — the sight of a half skeleton and half regular upholstered mule, bolting across the desert.*

11 *O wondrous is thy Divine Plan, O Lord, that could work in such an amazing skill. The Gaboon Adder really does make bees and wasps look pretty unimpressive by comparison. But yay, O Lord, that's not to say that bees and wasps weren't worth making in the first place; they are indeed splendid and mind-boggling creatures that give my son and me a great deal of pleasure (though I should point out, O Lord, that nothing untoward goes on with respect to the bees and wasps; it's all good clean fun — anything else would be mightily sinful and I don't go in for that sort of carry on at all. True*

Figure 15B: A Mobile Rosicrucian Milking Castle

Used in the mid to late 14th century, wheeled milking castles were powered by clockwork and sent into enemy territory harbouring Gaboon adders. Under the cover of night, trained monkeys would milk the snakes while they slept. These milking raids rarely went well. Usually the snakes would wake up and begin shrieking, and other animals (usually lemurs and geese but occasionally the odd rhinoceros) would defend the snakes' honour by charging the castle. The Mason-in-Charge would wind up the milking castle with a giant key and the monkeys would escape. Milking castles were banned by Martin Luther in 1521.

though it is that I once accidentally had sex with a bison – but that's another Confession).

Most scholars agree that this is the first recorded historical reference to what the Rosicrucian Order of the Masons would call 'TimeSerum'. Sadly, the Gaboon adder was eventually driven to extinction by excessive hunting, capture and milking; they were also highly prized as knee socks by the Wodaabe people.

The remaining venom was fiercely protected by the Rosicrucians. Indeed, a giant artesian well is thought to exist under Stonehenge containing enough TimeSerum to fill over two hundred Olympic-sized swimming pools, one of which is rumoured to have a diving board.

Chapter 13

IN WHICH OUR HERO IS SAVED BY
THE ROSICRUCIAN MONKS

15th day of January Anno Domini Iesu Christi 1658,
around lunch time, Streonaeshealh Abbey, Northumbria

ORAY AND LEEUWENHOEK DIS-mounted their goats outside the turreted monastery and Alexander Pruitt pulled the bell rope near the massive oak doors. A tart peal sounded in the distance, followed by sharp footsteps and coughing. Bolts rasped and chains fell, and the two doors heaved open to reveal a wraith-like figure in robes, who eyed the strangers suspiciously from within the shadow of its rough hessian hood.

The good doctor rocked backwards and forwards on his heels for a few moments as he was assessed. The lens grinder whistled tunelessly and, along with the Cromwell's-son-inhabiting-man-from-the-future, pretended to admire the rough stonework of the monastery walls. Apparently satisfied, the figure bid its guests enter, raising a bony finger to its lips as it did so. The three men followed their silent host inside the building, the echo of their footfalls rising in the great hall and scattering the doves hidden in the eaves.

With only a solitary candle festooned with ancient runes for illumination, the men sat in a cold stone room and discussed Alexander's plight. He wanted to go home, this much was understood. But how? After much *va-et-vient* it was determined that the ectomorphic abbot would administer the sleeping potion and conceal the deeply snoozing body in one of the myriad intertwining catacombs that lay under the monastery.

Elaborately coded instructions detailing the intricate how-tos of Alexander's revivification would be hidden and hidden again over the ensuing centuries, and when the time was right, the last generation of trusted guardians of the already unspeakably secret Royal Society would see to it that Alexander was woken and returned to his father's bosom.

Hands were shaken and oaths sworn all round as on that night began the beginning of a commencement that would start the very first in a series of a chain of events so cataclysmic that every other chain of cataclysmic events throughout history would look like a Pandora bracelet worn on the ankle of a very small fawn.

Over time, the secret society would grow and membership would spread across the globe. The slumbering form of Richard Cromwell/Alexander Pruitt would be moved from one covert cranny to another within any number of Masonic buildings throughout the land. As only the most elite cabal of Brethren would have access to the ciphers and maps divining the whereabouts of their charge, this exclusive order came to be named after the simple apprentice monk who first hid the inert, though still slightly snoring, doppelganger of Richard Cromwell: Rogerites.

An enormous fart rent the air and all heads spun around to see a filthy bearded shambles step out from a sulphurous cloud. Roger was pushing a small wooden trolley. The skeleton excused itself from Moray and Leeuwenhoek, and clattered over to speak with its associate.

'Kan vee trust dese mens?' whispered Leeuwenhoek.

'We have no choice,' Moray whispered back. 'We must undo what we have done – for his sake.'

The Scot looked down fondly at his sleeping patient and stroked his hair. 'Goodnight, lad.'

'Do yoo zink vee shood take hiz trousess off before dey file him avay?' asked Leeuwenhoek.

'Excuse me?'

'Vell, for de medikal porpoises, yoo understant.'

'No, that won't be necessary.'

A filthy bearded shambles stepped out
from a sulphurous cloud.

'All pervectly aboff de boards …'

'He'll be fine. Leave his trousers alone.'

'I'm vorried he shood ged a strankulation frum hiz trousess—'

'I said no.'

'Dat's why vee all vear das pyjammaz, yoo knoe—'

'I *know* why we wear pyjamas.'[18]

The overly concerned Dutchman was still justifying his pants-removal suggestion as they rode away from the monastery but Moray's thoughts were elsewhere. Suddenly, the doctor's face turned ashen and an involuntary high-pitched squeak emanated from his voice box.

'Dear God, what have we done?!' he exclaimed as he pulled hard on his reins, forcing his goat to rear up. Moray cantered back to the monastery to speak to the skeleton, which was still waving them goodbye from the tower.

---

18. Pyjamas were first worn during the French Revolution by King Louis XVII and were invented by Buzz Aldrin. The name derives from the Hindi word *malpaso*, which means 'to invest heavily in cardboard'. *Ref.* Wikipedia.

'I've just realised something,' he called up to the emaciated monk. 'If that young man is revived in the future, it will be a future in which he was never born! I will have never implanted a twig of Richard Cromwell in his mother's womb, and his father will not know him!'

The skeleton looked confused, and rightly so.

'We have to wake him up!' yelled Moray, as a panting Leeuwenhoek joined him. 'When he awakes in AD 2005, he will be as alone as he ever was in this time!'

'But we've already filed him away in the catacombs—' protested the calcium-rich abbot.

'In the name of the King and God himself,' thundered Moray with as much gravitas as he could while sitting astride a goat, 'I command you to waken Alexander Pruitt!'

The skeleton shrugged and pulled on the bell rope next to him. A neat stack of campanologs later, and the bedraggled Roger was standing by his side on the battlements.

'Do you remember where you put the Unconscious One?' he asked his lowly apprentice.

Roger bowed low, lost his balance and toppled over the stone balustrade to his death, the secret of Alexander Pruitt's whereabouts dying with him.

'Oh, shuzbut!' exclaimed the skeleton.

&

AND SO IT WAS RESOLVED THAT DOCTOR Robert Fenwick Aloysius Moray would be administered the venom of the Gaboon adder and filed away in the catacombs of Lodge No. 1, there to lie until the advance of science would enable him to implant the cells from Richard Cromwell into the eggs of Charlie Pruitt's wife. But while Alexander would have a family to return to when he awoke, Doctor Moray could never go back to his own time. In effect, he was sacrificing his future so that Alexander could have a past.

It was a selfless act of kindness that, over the centuries, Moray would come to regret, one that ultimately would change the very face of history itself.

On the way down the mountain, having bid adieu to his old friend, Leeuwenhoek was seized by his own notion. Before it could fully articulate itself in his mind, however, the man from the Netherlands was set upon and arrested

by the much-feared and loathed Guards of
the Lord Protector. Widow Makepeace had
blabbed. The Dutch aesthete was clapped in
irons and thrown into the dankest dungeon
that Cromwell's castle could oblige.

Chapter 14

*17th day of September Iesu Christi 2005,
14:30:22 post meridiem GMT, Las Vegas, Nevada*

OUG HENNING PACED AROUND his dressing room in a denim bathrobe, puffing away on an enormous post-show spliff.

'Why'd ya have to bring Cruise along?' he complained. 'These Masonic zombie rituals ain't part of my regular show, you know. I don't want no goddamn celebrity audience.'

I explained that Tom wanted to play me in a movie version of the book I was writing, and was here for research purposes.

'Movie, eh?' mumbled the magician, stopping to regard himself in the mirror. 'Who's playing me?'

'That depends,' I teased, 'on just how successful you are at resurrecting the late Mr Pruitt.'

Henning took a quick step towards me – leaving behind him a thick cloud of ganja in the exact shape of his body – and raised his finger threateningly. 'I don't want to see no David Copperfield wearing buckteeth and a wig. It's Jeremy Irons or I'm out.'

I demurred. Tom was likely to have casting approval and at that moment he was down the corridor practising karate moves with some Elvis impersonators. What I wanted to know was whether Doug Henning could really raise the dead.

The master illusionist took a final drag on his doobie, grabbed the smoke as he exhaled and then slowly opened his hand to reveal that it had … disappeared.[19]

'It was just a regular Las Vegas matinee,' he said mysteriously. 'A crowd of Jap tourists and old ladies keen to witness what the posters out front promised would be an afternoon of "thrilling magic, the likes of which they'd never seen before". What they got instead was "spattered in blood".'

I sat there, agog, as Henning spilt the beans.

---

19. The smoke, not his hand.

What they got instead was "spattered in blood".

'As that white Siberian tiger sunk its fangs into Roy,' Doug continued, 'Siegfried went into a kinda trance. When I jumped onto that stage and sliced poor old Montecore in two with my sword, he didn't move, barely batted so much as an eyelid as I scooped out Roy's remains and used my powers to bring him back to life ... *And* I got rid of the chew marks.'

Amazing.

'It musta been some sort of epiphany. Two weeks later, Siggy goes down to the flea market under the Hoover Dam Bypass Bridge and sells all their stuff – everything they ever owned, spread out on a table at a swap meet. Can you believe it? By the time Roy gets home they're a million bucks richer, but out of showbiz and running a Wendy's on Durango Drive.'

Incredible.

'One of the things they sold was this—' whispered Doug, producing from the deep folds of his sleeve a small book, which he presented to me with a theatrical bow. It was a leather-bound volume of letters written by Sir Arthur Conan Doyle to a certain Mr Harry Houdini.

Somewhere down the hallway could be heard the clatter of a fire-extinguisher as it was kicked off the wall by Tom Cruise, followed by the sycophantic laughter of Elvises. But I was too engrossed to notice.[20]

'Both guys were into Spiritualism big time, you know, and they became pals,' Doug explained. 'Those letters you got there were purchased by Zachary J. Loomis of Weehawken, New Jersey, for $12,700.' Doug paused a moment. 'Excuse me, won't you?' He stepped behind a screen and changed into a fresh pair of bright blue overalls with an embroidered cat on the bib. He had a matinee in five minutes.

'Now Loomis was an unemployed carpet-tile layer and money's kinda tight ...' the

---

20. In fact, I don't know why I mentioned it really.

magician continued. 'So that night he and his old lady argue about the bread and a couple of chairs get thrown. The broad goes crazy loco, you dig? So Loomis says I'm outta here, packs his bags and splits.' Doug was now before the mirror, combing his moustache. 'When I meet this Loomis dame in her brownstone flea trap a month later, she was a no good stinkin' drunk and I got that book of letters from her for next to nothin'.' He smiled, and looked over the reflection of his shoulder at the reflection of me sitting behind him holding a reflection of the book. 'Consider them a gift – and a demonstration of my bona fides.'

And with that, he … disappeared.[21]

---

21. Through the door.

HOTEL METROPOLE
28 MARITIME CRES., ROTTINGDEAN, BRIGHTON BN, ENGLAND
MAJOR (RET.) L. Q. SPONK, PROP.

13th October 1888

Mr H. Houdini
Empire Theatre
430 Broadway/40th St
Manhattan
NY, USA

Dearest Harry,

My lady friend and I are enjoying the sea baths here.
They are wet and invigorating, with much to recommend
them in terms of their moistness and revitalising
properties. My own energies have, of late, been
particularly sapped and are in dire need of soddening
and de-enervation.

You may recall that when I last wrote to you it was of
the terrible Whitechapel Murders. Two women thus far
- each strangled in the dead of night and hideously
mutilated. As expected, the newspapers were full
of lurid speculation as to the likely culprit. (One
yellow daily even published a letter of confession
from the supposed MURDERER HIMSELF!!!) I would have
kept you apprised of each hysterical development as
it unfurled were it not for an unusual commission I
received, which, regrettably forced my correspondence
on the subject to an abrupt end. You could be excused
for thinking me rude, my dear friend, and I hope

the following goes some way to assuage you of this
impression and restore our good relations.

After the second murder, I received a telegram from
the Chief-Superintendent of the City Police, Sir
Charles Warren, seeking my help. It was not the first
time - nor, I suspect, would it be the last - that the
remarkable sleuthing abilities of my fictional Holmes
were to be mistaken for my own far less impressive
talents. Sir Charles, as you know, is a Fellow and
although I am perhaps a fair-weather Fellow myself,
I hastened as requested to Great Scotland Yard for a
meeting.

Even a cursory glance at the police photos suggested
at least a nod to 17th-century Masonic ritual in the
slayings. Instantly, my mind went back to an incident a
full year before, when H. G. Wells and I were visiting
the Quatuor Coronati Lodge No. 2076 (where Sir Charles
is the First Master). We were there in the capacity
of spectators to a seldom-performed ceremony called
Anadi Mortuum, a laughable piece of music hall that
eventually turned quite blood curdling. At the time,
neither Wells nor I believed that the 'corpse' (so
still, we had initially taken it to be a wax mannequin)
lying on the altar with tubes running into him from a
metal box on his chest could be RAISED FROM THE DEAD!!!

Wells and I had shaken hands with the actor - a man
named Robert Moray - and congratulated him on a most
convincing performance. A remarkable actor, yes - but
only an actor, after all. Yet there he was in the
photograph Sir Charles was showing to me: a suspect in
these dreadful Ripper Murders.

Moray had remained in character throughout his
conversation with Wells and me: a creditable
impersonation of a physician from the Court of
Charles I with an outlandish tale worthy of Rip Van
Winkle. He had been, he said, asleep for more than
two hundred years. All good fun. Or so we thought.

Sir Charles advised me that Moray was working at the
London Lock Hospital and was now the Chief Surgeon
of the new gynaecological wards opened last May by
Dr Gull, Physician to Her Majesty. He also advised me
of something not hitherto known about the Ripper's
victims - that Mary Ann Nichols and Annie Chapman had
both been pregnant to at least their first trimestris
and that the mutilations they had suffered had taken
place so that the unborn foeti could be removed. The
startling news, however, was that both women had been
patients of Dr Moray.

It is late and I shall write more of this adventure
tomorrow. Melodramatic of me to leave off now, I know.
It's a hangover from working for The Strand that I
cannot shake.

Your respectful servant and friend,

Arthur Conan Doyle.

Chapter 15

IN WHICH TOM REVEALS HIS PLAN

17th day of September Anno Domini Iesu Christi 2005,
18:53:57 post meridiem GMT, New Mexico

E WERE RACING ALONG AN UNSEALED road somewhere in the New Mexico Desert when the drugs began to wear off. All that passive smoking in Doug Henning's dressing room had made it difficult for me to tell where we were going, but I sure as hell knew it wasn't back to the Holiday Inn. Even Tom, who'd only been exposed to the third-hand fumes wafting off my jacket, had all but blacked out when we hit Death Valley Junction.

By the time we pulled up at the security gate of what looked to be some sort of top-level military installation, Cruise was alert and back to his old ebullient self. He gave a wink and finger-pistol shot at the guard, who saluted him and waved the limo through. Hubbard tilted a little as the car lurched onto a smaller access road and Cruise reached across me to steady him. 'Got a bit of a surprise for ya,' he confided with a taut grin of porcelain implants.

I was beginning to feel uncomfortable – and it wasn't just because I was sandwiched between a dead man and Tom Cruise.

After being waved through another security gate inside the perimeter – one that bore a huge sign declaring we were entering 'Area 51' – we came to a stop at a reserved parking bay outside a large aircraft hangar.

Cruise looked at me with smouldering dead eyes. 'What you're about to see,' he intoned in a low voice that didn't sound like his but, judging by the vague synchronisation with his lip movements, was, 'you must never divulge to anyone.' He paused for effect and then gripped my arm. 'I GODDAMN mean it, dude.'

'Okay, I promise.'

'SWEAR IT!!!'

'Yeah, yeah – I swear,' I whined, trying to unfasten his perfectly manicured fingers from my elbow. 'I won't tell a soul—'

'You better not, pal …' Cruise glanced up to meet the eyes of the chauffeur in the rear-vision mirror, then returned his attention to mine. He held my incredulous look with his frozen stare for a moment, then exploded into laughter. 'I'm just messin' with you, man. You're all right – you know that? YEAH!'

Cruise was laughing so hard that veins began to bulge on his temples. He mussed my hair and shadow-boxed at me for a few seconds. Then, as the massive hangar door slid open, the merriment drained from his face like a blob of mercury sliding off a Teflon slippery-dip.

Cruise strode purposefully ahead of me and into the hangar as a grid of fluoros flickered on. My eyes were still acclimatising to the light when he spun around, waving energetically at the huge flying saucer–shaped tarpaulin in the centre of the room.

'You know what this is?' Cruise asked, his booming voice bouncing off the metal walls and ceiling.

I was about to say, 'It's pretty obviously a flying saucer,' when he grabbed a guy rope and swirled the protective cover away with a matador flourish to reveal what lay beneath:

Cruise judo-kicked at the surface a few times.

a flying saucer. One of those really clichéd 1950s-looking ones.

'A flying FREAKIN' saucer, man!' announced the diminutive megastar, with as much drama as the already deflated situation and his limited acting ability would allow.

Cruise explained that the saucer had crash-landed in Roswell in 1947, and that L. Ron

Hubbard had been working with the US Government to unlock its secrets and, indeed, the craft itself. It had no doors or windows; no seams or hinges; no way of getting in or out – it seemed to be just one massive piece of impenetrable metal. Cruise judo-kicked at the surface a few times to demonstrate how impregnable it was.

'I've only ever seen pictures of aliens on the internet,' I told Cruise over the clanging. 'Surely they're not real.'

Cruise delivered a coup de grâce, which almost fractured his ankle, and laughed. '*Everything* on the internet is true, man,' he assured me. 'Except the stuff about me – particularly that goddamn YouTube footage from Oprah.'

According to Cruise, when the military had turned up to investigate the crash, they'd found two of the aliens underneath the saucer, trying to repair it. The Pentagon had ordered their immediate capture, interrogation and dissection. The extensive grilling and exhaustive autopsies revealed nothing, and the bodies were buried in the Arizona desert, near where the opening title sequence for *The*

New Dick Van Dyke Show had been shot.[22]

Both Strategic Air Command and the Scientologists hoped that by utilising the process of reverse engineering, the secrets to eternal life would finally be revealed to Man and L. Ron Hubbard could be revived. The plan was that he would take over the Scientology paperwork, thus freeing up Cruise to assume his rightful position as the terrestrial manifestation of the dictator of the Galactic Confederacy, Xenu.

'But that means … you don't want to make my book into a film at all,' I spluttered, backing away. 'You just want to know about that 400-year-old man I found in France.'

'Who's to say this can't be a win-win situation for both of us?' countered Cruise, as he advanced. 'You get your movie … I get to rule the Universe.'

---

22. In fact, if you freeze-frame that opening title sequence at 0.78 seconds you can see, in the background, a brief flash of an alien climbing out of his grave, noticing the camera and then ducking back down again. As a result, Dick Van Dyke was subsequently arrested, interrogated and dissected, but no new evidence resulted. He was replaced with a look-alike robot so he could appear to star in *Diagnosis: Murder*.

I half stumbled over some electrical cables.

'One thing I don't understand though ...' said Cruise, tilting his head a little.

'Oh yeah – what's ... what's that?' I was trying to humour him, to buy myself some time.

'I get the whole, you know, Gonzo historian thing,' he said, getting closer. 'But the switching from Omniscient Narrator to First Person Narrator confuses me.'

I almost lost my footing on some widgets but steadied myself on a drum. 'Well, you see, it's actually the same narrator all the way through,' I explained. 'It's just that sometimes I'm writing from my own experience and other times it's from my research or what people have told me—'

Cruise kicked away the widgets and they clattered across the hard concrete floor. 'But the level of detail you have in the historical material – how could you know?'

'It's a standard device in creative non-fiction,' I rambled, reaching behind me, hopeful of finding the hangar door. 'Have you read Norman Mailer's *The Castle in the Forest*?'

'I have the audio-book version on my iPod,' said Cruise. 'I think Ray Liotta reads it ...'

I turned and broke into a sprint for the door, only to find it locked. Frantically, I called for help.

'Yell all you want, man; no-one can hear you,' said Cruise calmly. 'I had this joint soundproofed by Phil Spector.' To prove his point, he joined me at the door and started pummelling it with his little fists and whooping like a baboon.

'Everything okay in there, Mr Cruise?' asked his chauffeur from outside.

'Goddamn Spector, man,' snarled the Hollywood A-lister. 'If he ever gets outta the big house, I'm suing his donkey-cornflake ass—'

'SHOW ME THE MONEY!' I yelled involuntarily.

Cruise bid me shut up with a vague karate-chop hand gesture and returned his attention to his unseen driver. 'Yeah, no – we're cool in here, man. Thanks.'

'Are you sure, Mr Cruise?' continued the concerned manservant. ''Cos there's, like, thirty or forty armed men in flak jackets out here wantin' to know what's goin' on …'

'Have they got CIA written on their backs in big yellow letters?'

'Hang on, I'll check …' There was a pause. Then there wasn't. 'Er … yeah.'

Cruise muttered a discreet 'freak' under his breath, squatted down and pulled open a drainage grate. 'Don't try and follow me, mofo, or I'll have my robot army hunt you down and give you an R6 Implant, capiche?'

I did. And with that Cruise disappeared into the hole, pulling the grating back over himself as the hangar door slid open and the blinding desert sun streamed in.

Half an hour later, I was shackled to a pole on a Hercules military transport, bound for rendition somewhere in Africa.

Tom Cruise, on the other hand, and within the same half-hour, climbed out of a stormwater pipe on the Universal lot, covered in rat faeces, and went straight into shooting another movie. Unfortunately for audiences, it was *War of the Worlds*.

Chapter 16

IN WHICH THE CHURCH IS IMPLICATED

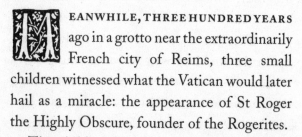

EANWHILE, THREE HUNDRED YEARS ago in a grotto near the extraordinarily French city of Reims, three small children witnessed what the Vatican would later hail as a miracle: the appearance of St Roger the Highly Obscure, founder of the Rogerites.

The children had been innocently stoning frogs when the long-dead seventeenth-century monk descended from the clouds to the sounds of a heavenly choir – and the squeaks of what some sceptics suggest was 'a winch or pulley system' – and gave the youngsters a map, which, he said, '... would lead them to something greater than treasure ...' He then farted horribly and disappeared.

A report filed with local police on the same day has St Roger turning up later that afternoon in a nearby convent and exposing himself to noviciates, but this is unsubstantiated and possibly was just the gardener.

The young trio were excited beyond belief, and raced from the grotto across a meadow to their homes, eager to tell their families of the mystical visitation they had received. On their way through hill and dale, however, a fierce storm broke over them and their heads were struck by a three-pronged fork of lightning. Two of the children were instantly incinerated, but the youngest, a three-year-old girl with a severe learning difficulty, was, mercifully, rendered mute, deaf, blind and paralysed from the bridge of her nose down.

The young girl was cared for around the clock by nuns – who revered her and believed her inertia to be a manifestation of Godliness. Constant prayers and an inferno of votive candles later, and she was, one afternoon several years later, able to move the little finger of her right hand a fraction of an inch.

It was a miracle!

The parish priest was called. Crowds gathered. Civic receptions were held. The Pope himself visited from Rome. The anti-Pope, too, rode in from Avignon. It was all settled: the little girl was to get her own Feast Day and preparations were made to announce her beatification.

Then the fishing line was discovered.

A well-intentioned, but misguided, altar boy was given a serious dressing down by both his Holiness and his anti-Holiness, and the paralysed child was officially branded a heretic. As the Papal and anti-Papal entourages swept from the village in high dudgeon, a single tear fell from the little girl's eye.

The crestfallen altar boy witnessed this second miracle and called for the Popes to return and reconsider. The girl's tear was collected in a glass vial and examined by a

raft of cardinals and anti-cardinals. Both groups huddled in the village square and conferred. The Popes nodded and stroked their chins in thought. Then they stroked *each other's* chins and thought some more. They finally shook hands and were about to pronounce the girl a saint when Old Bodkin, the town apothecary, bid them wait; he had one last test to carry out.

The Popes nodded and stroked their chins in thought.

Old Bodkin hobbled over to the Holy and Unholy Fathers, carefully took the vial from them and repaired to his laboratory. He returned in a thrice, smacking his gums, and announced that the so-called 'tear' tasted a lot like urine. All eyes turned to the rather guilty-looking altar boy, who, after adjusting his surplice, ran away and hid in a chimney.

The Popes left for good, but no blame was directed towards the horizontal child. In an outpouring of sympathy and love, the townsfolk took up a collection and sent the young girl on a holiday to visit the Abbey at Monte Cassino. It all went well apart from the murder.

St Roger's map was sealed in the altar of the local parish church for almost one hundred years. It was reputed to have special healing powers. Indeed, a young miller's daughter claimed that her gonorrhoea, which had mysteriously appeared the day after her wedding night, miraculously changed, after a prayer vigil, into syphilis.

Towards the turn of the nineteenth century, Neo-Goths sacked the church and stole the lead from the roof, later selling it to black-market radiologists for use in their protective aprons.

St Roger's map disappeared and was feared lost. It next turned up in the family papers of Sir Arthur Conan Doyle's grandfather, who couldn't make a lick of sense out of it. That is until ...[23]

---

23. I thought these dots were a neat dramatic device to create some suspense. Hopefully, it hasn't been dissipated by this footnote.

Chapter 17

IN WHICH THE RIPPER STRIKES AGAIN

30th day of September Anno Domini Iesu Christi 1888,
21:34:11 post meridiem GMT,
Great Scotland Yard, St James's, Westminster

LEXANDER PRUITT SAT BOLT upright and gasped at the air with such force that it hurt. The splendid moustaches of the two men who had revived him twitched like epileptic millipedes.

Another man, who wore an even more splendid moustache, but with decidedly less animation about it, watched from his desk on the other side of the room. Alexander was still trying to get his bearings when the man marched over to get a better look at him.

'Well, 'e certainly looks alive,' said the gent, squinting over an imaginary pair of glasses and poking at Alexander with his fountain pen. 'But what can 'e tell us of these dreadful murders?'

As it turned out, not much.

Alexander explained to the moustachioed men that he was supposed to have been revived in the year 2005. Someone, he claimed, was 117 years out.

The owner of one of the lesser moustaches, Sir Arthur Conan Doyle, apologised on behalf of the Sacred Order of Rogerites, of which he was Honorary Capstan. The other, H. G. Wells – a lowly subaltern from the same group, but a great chum of Conan Doyle's – explained, with great speed, the nature of the emergency.

'Jack the Ripper?' Alexander repeated to himself. It didn't seem possible.

'You have 'eard of him, then?' quizzed the owner of the greater and more relaxed moustache, Inspector Lestrade of Scotland Yard.

'I've heard of him, yes – in books ...'

Lestrade snorted and turned away. 'Heard about 'im in books, 'ave you now? What books would these be then, eh?'

'Books from the future, Inspector,' offered H. G. Wells earnestly.

Lestrade had had quite enough. He hurled his fountain pen angrily across the room and turned on the famous authors. 'I know all about your books, Mr Wells,' he barked. 'I've read all about your so-called "Time Machines" and your "Martian Invasions" and your "Voyages to the Bottom of the Sea"—'

'I think you'll find that last one was by Jules Verne—' interrupted Wells.

'Don't interrupt!' snapped Lestrade. 'Whether you wrote 'em or not, they're all the same – the lot of 'em. All confections, every one; little treats to satisfy the sweet tooth of the simpletons who'd rather lose themselves in the fancies of cloud-cuckoo-land than live in the real world—'

'See here, Lestrade – that's a bit strong. We're only trying to—'

'And I've 'ad quite enough of you too, Mr Arthur Bloody Conan Bloody Doyle,' further vented the Inspector. 'It's not enough you appropriate my good name for your so-called detective stories, you 'ave to reduce me to some music 'all copper 'oo can barely speak the Queen's English, such is 'is thick 'nd almost impenetr'ble Cockney accent.' The aggrieved peeler drew himself up to his full height of five feet seven inches and held his finger in the air, imperiously. 'For 'e 'oo felches me purse felches only me cash, but 'e 'oo felches me good name felches something very valuable indeed.' And with that, he brought his fist down on the ink blotter with a finality that sent his pencils flying off in all directions.

It was a few seconds before the pencils stopped falling down the backs of filing cabinets and bouncing off the windowsill. This, plus the fact that Lestrade had failed to retract his pointing finger as he smashed his fist onto the desk, considerably lessened the theatrical force of the gesture. Nonetheless, it was clear that Lestrade had finished his upbraid and the two authors were left speechless in its wake.

What follows would have been a very dull paragraph indeed, what with all three men standing around saying nothing, had it not been for the arrival of PC Abercrombie Jones, breathless and sweating, and full of news.

❧

WITH LESTRADE LEADING THE WAY, CONAN Doyle trundling a still-groggy Alexander Pruitt in a bath chair and the more portly Wells waddling up the rear, the four men

Outside a grim hovel stood a fearful constable.

trailed along after PC Abercrombie Jones as he forged through the fog to a dank alley off the Whitechapel Road. Only on a Monopoly board would this street fetch as much as sixty pounds. In real life, you wouldn't bother putting your hand in your pocket for such a foul and squalid stretch of road – unless to pull out a revolver.

Outside a grim hovel stood a fearful constable. He saluted Lestrade as he passed and shot a quizzical glance at PC Abercrombie Jones as the Inspector's motley entourage passed through the doorway.

Inside, all was dark but for a fitful candle guttering on the rotting table in the centre of the room. As it danced, splashes of blood were illuminated on the wall. On the bed lay the remains of the Ripper's latest victim.

Conan Doyle, a medical man, felt for a pulse on the wrist of a severed arm, then shook his head sadly. Wells steadied himself by grabbing onto the mantelpiece and, despite all efforts to the contrary, vomited copiously into the fireplace.

'Gawd!' exclaimed the landlord, wearing a grim expression and a grimy apron. 'Another bleedin' mess to clean up …'

Conan Doyle flushed red and raised his cane to the man but Lestrade stayed his hand. 'Don't you think there's been enough violence in this 'ouse tonight, Sir Arthur?' the lawman chided.

'Excuse me, Guv'nor,' PC Abercrombie Jones interrupted from the doorway. 'I think you'd better come and have a look at this …'

The men gathered around the police constable as he held up his lantern to a spot on the crumbling wall. There – written in blood – were the following words:

THE JUWES ARE NOT THE
MEN THAT WILL BE BLAMED
FOR NOTHING

'Curious,' began Conan Doyle. 'Whoever wrote this is suggesting that Jews *won't* be the men who people will blame for not doing anything.'

'Not for "not doing anything",' corrected Wells. 'But for *nothing* at all.'

Conan Doyle brushed the overside of his finger across his moustache. 'True – but why declare that someone *won't* be accused of the *absence* of something?'

'Perhaps it was to confuse us,' chipped in the police constable.

'Shut up, Jones,' admonished Lestrade.

'No, no, Inspector – the constable is right.' And here Conan Doyle folded his arms, and rested his chin between the thumb and forefinger of his right hand. 'A double negative has been employed here in order to force us to waste valuable time in deciphering it.' He leaned forward and studied the words more closely. 'What the message really says – if you cancel out the double negative—'

'Or *deux négatif*, as they would say in *la belle France*,' added Wells pointlessly.

'Is …' here Conan Doyle corrugated his brow a little, 'the Jews *are* the men who *will* be blamed for nothing.'

'Still doesn't make any sense,' muttered Lestrade.

The others agreed.

'Perhaps it's a *triple* positive,' croaked Alexander Pruitt from the darkness. He rose unsteadily from his bath chair and, leaning on H. G. Wells' shoulder, descended to one knee in order to take in the message. 'Perhaps whoever wrote this is saying that the Jews *are* the men who *will* be blamed for *something*.'

There were murmurs of assent all round.

Even from the landlord in the grimy apron, who shouldn't really have been listening.

'But blamed for *what*?' asked the PC.

Lestrade almost hit the young constable with his truncheon. 'What d'ya think "for *what*"? These bleedin' murders, of course!'

'Not necessarily,' volunteered Wells, adding a note of caution.

'Wot?' blustered an exasperated Lestrade. 'So, it doesn't mean anything, then?' The Inspector was just about ready to give the game up entirely and retire to a life of beekeeping in Dorset.

It was Wells' turn to hold court, something he didn't get to do too often with Conan Doyle around. 'Let us not forget that the purpose of the message is merely to throw us off the scent. The murderer wants us to waste valuable time debating the meaning of the message while he makes good his escape. He commits the crime, writes a meaningless message on the wall in his victim's blood and hopes we'll come along and be so distracted by it that we'll become completely preoccupied and forget that we should, in fact, be out there chasing the fiend.'

'And meanwhile, the trail of the Ripper grows cold,' ruminated Lestrade, a tinge of admiration in his voice. 'Very clever. Very bloody clever indeed.'

'Of course!' agreed Sir Arthur, clapping his partners-in-crime-solving on their respective shoulders. 'And while we're standing around simultaneously congratulating ourselves on being able to divine the true meaning of the madman's message and dipping our lid to his cunning and guile, the chances of actually capturing the brute become ever more remote.'

'Not only that,' added PC Abercrombie Jones, 'but even when we realise that the message is simply a ruse to distract us, we get sidetracked into believing the message and thinking that the murderer is in fact giving us a clue: *viz*, that someone is going to blame the Jews for these murders.'

'When, in fact, it's not the Jews at all – but the complete opposite.'

All eyes turned to Alexander Pruitt, who was still bent on one knee, unable to get up.

'You mean …' Lestrade's unfinished question hung in the air like a herring pegged to a clothesline.

'Exactly!' affirmed Alexander with an economy that turned out to be rather unhelpful, as nobody knew what he meant.

'The Freemasons,' he added, for clarity's sake.

The landlord in the grimy apron turned to the coalman next to him. 'You 'eard 'im,' he whispered coarsely. 'Let's get them Jews!' And with that, the two men stole away, assembled a mob and burned down all the shops in East Finchley.

Conan Doyle nodded gravely. 'Yes, yes – although let us not tar all those in our Brotherhood with this disgraceful brush.' He gestured to Alexander. 'Our undead friend speaks of one Mason in particular, a man whose membership in our organisation should be seriously reconsidered when next his subs are due ...'

'A *Mason* did these terrible deeds?' questioned an appalled Lestrade. 'Surely you can't be—'

'That's exactly what I—' countered the learned author, interrupting himself with a significant pause, which, on closer analysis, turned out to be of no significance at all.

'These murders could not *only* have been carried out by a Mason – but *also* by a crazed madman or some sort of … monster. Perhaps both.'

'Copycat killer, eh, Conan Doyle?' said an interjecting Wells knowingly, wildly missing several points.

'Not at all,' rejoindered Conan Doyle. 'I speak of none other than Doctor Robert Fenwick Aloysius Moray, personal physician to Her Majesty, Victoria Regina.'

PC Abercrombie Jones laughed out loud, thinking 'Regina' sounded a bit rude, before Inspector Lestrade hit him with his own truncheon.

❧

HER MAJESTY HERSELF WAS NOT AT ALL amused when roused from her sleep by her equerry to be told that several policemen, assorted authors and a revived clone of Oliver Cromwell's son wished to have urgent talks with her in the palace garden. In fact, the equerry left the last bit out, as he thought the situation was outlandish enough as it was.

The Queen put on her corsets, best dressing gown and slippers and padded downstairs and out the French windows.

'What do you mean one's personal physician is a psychopath?' asked England's longest-serving monarch, upon being told by Inspector Lestrade that her personal physician was a psychopath.

'I don't know that I can make it any more clear, Ma'am,' answered the policeman a tad naughtily.

Her Majesty turned to Sir Arthur for help. She had a dim memory of once anointing his shoulders with a sword, and therefore trusted him. He explained as best he could about the cloning, the soul transference, the Gaboon adder, St Roger, etc, but it was a lot to take in and the Queen, who wasn't very smart and barely spoke English, was very confused. She sat down, totally bamboozled, on the head of a stone lion, and bid her equerry go and wake her son Edward.

The police and authors rolled their eyes as discreetly as they could. There was considerable scepticism that the half-mad and incredibly stupid Prince would be able to make things any easier to understand.

Prince Edward listened intently as Lestrade, Sir Arthur, H. G. Wells, Alexander Pruitt, PC Abercrombie Jones and even the equerry gave their versions of events over and over again. Eventually, he claimed to understand what was going on and recounted his distillation of their accounts to his mother in her native tongue. There was quite a bit of *sturm* and *drang*.

The Queen's eyes lit up, turned fearful, went calm and became vacant at various bits of the story. When Edward was through, he had worked himself into such a Germanic lather that the equerry had to throw a bucket of water over him. He lay gurgling in the puddle while Her Majesty signed Moray's death warrant.

'It saddens one,' the Queen announced as she returned her quill to the inkwell, 'that Doctor Moray must die. He was the finest chiropodist one has ever had tend to one's corns.'

Inspector Lestrade nodded with as much mock sympathy as he dared and relieved the old Queen of the document. The equerry poured some blotting powder on it – rather too much, in fact – and it was only after the cloud had cleared that it became apparent to those thanking the Monarch that Her Majesty had already retired upstairs.

The men had a job to do and had been charged by the highest authority in the land to expedite it with all speed. They stepped resolutely over the Prince of Wales, now fast asleep in his puddle, and into the Royal Carriage the Queen had generously left at their disposal. With the crack of a whip and a tumble of hooves, the game was afoot.

※

MEANWHILE, ACCORDING TO A CHAIN of fishwives, night-soil collectors, opium eaters, strumpets and other grubby witnesses, the Ripper's trail wended its way to London's fog-laden Limehouse area. Holed up in a Chinese laundry at the end of the docks that night was the demented Moray, covered in filth and blood.

Chapter 18

❧

*29th day of June Anno Domini Iesu Christi 1658,
brunch, Huntingdon, East Anglia*

HAINED TO THE WALL IN HIS CELL,
Leeuwenhoek could not escape the
agonised screams of the Widow
Makepeace. They pierced the dungeon air
like a lance tied onto the hood of Donald
Campbell's Bluebird-Proteus CN7. At any
moment the old woman would crack and
name names, and Leeuwenhoek would be in
even bigger trouble.

The screams grew louder as she was dragged
past his door, then there was silence either
side of a distant splash somewhere beyond his
small barred window.

All of a sudden the heavy wooden door to
Leeuwenhoek's damp cell swung open and in

walked the Witchfinder-General, Matthew Hopkins. In one of his impressively gloved hands he held an unfurled parchment; in the other, a still-smouldering white-hot branding-iron in the shape of Oliver Cromwell. Behind him stood the real Oliver Cromwell himself.

'Before she was drowned, the late widow was most forthcoming,' purred Cromwell as Hopkins blew on the parchment a little to help the ink dry. 'She told us some *verrrrry* interesting things about you, my old Dutchman.'

Leeuwenhoek struggled impotently in his shackles as the Lord Protector began to laugh and the Witchfinder-General danced about with glee on the straw-strewn floor. Cromwell looked on approvingly as his most trusted Minister, bedecked from head to toe in the stygian black clerical garb for which he was known and feared, flapped about like some giant mad bat. He joined Hopkins in a rudimentary frug, but as the potential sinfulness of their rug-cutting dawned on them, they both came to a stop as suddenly as they had begun and looked about suspiciously in case anyone had seen. There was no-one but Leeuwenhoek, and he would soon be dead.

Figure 28K: Matthew Hopkins Witchfinder-General, 1659
Matthew Hopkins posed for this woodcut shortly after being elected. It was a particularly difficult woodcut as the animals kept wandering off. Hopkins patiently posed for just under six months. As his office of Witchfinder only lasted six months, this left him one day to actually try any cases. Unfortunately, that day was his RDO. We don't know the name of his replacement, nor do we have a picture of him.

'I now know all I need to know about soul transference …' announced Cromwell offhandedly, bending down to pluck an errant tuft of hay from his buckled shoe. 'So all Matthew and I need from you are the secrets of Morpheus—' he smiled a smile that made Basil Rathbone look like Bindi Irwin, and leaned in close to the manacled lens grinder as he continued, in a low whisper, 'which you through some unholy contract with Beelzebub hath learned.'

Leeuwenhoek gulped. 'Orr vat?' he trembled.

The Lord Protector's smile suddenly went missing. He looked around at Hopkins, who shrugged, and then back at Leeuwenhoek. '"Vat"?' he repeated. 'Is that what you said?'

'Yah – vat iv I doint tell yah what yoo vant to nose?'

Cromwell's face crumpled a bit. 'What? What I *what*?'

'Vant! Vant!' The prisoner was frantic.

'Are you saying "*want*"?'

'Yah, *vant*! Vat yoo *vant* to nose!'

The penny was dropping, but through a jar of molasses. 'Ah, I see – you're asking what happens if you don't tell me what I want to know?'

After a successful appeal, the sentence was
commuted to being burned at the stake.

'Yah, yah!' affirmed Leeuwenhoek, almost overjoyed. 'If I nod tell yoo vat yoo vant to nose … Vat habbens?'

Cromwell again gave his best Ultra-Rathbone and nodded to the Witchfinder-General, who raised the branding-iron to within a centimetre of his prisoner's unfortunate conk.

'If you don't tell the Lord Protector what he wants to *nose*,' taunted Hopkins, 'then you may find yourself without a *nose* of your own.' There was a malevolent sneer from the Witchfinder-General and another eruption of laughter from Cromwell that shook the very rafters and made the prisoner in the upstairs cell bang on his floor with a broom.

Needless to say, Leeuwenhoek told them everything he knew. Thereafter, he signed a confession and went to trial, whereafter the Judge, having heard all the evidence, ordered that Leeuwenhoek be taken from the court, weighted down by giant stones and hurled into a pond. After a successful appeal, the sentence was commuted to being burned at the stake. It helps to have a canny lawyer.

❧

IN THE MEANTIME, SEVERAL HUNDRED YEARS later, I, too, had my own torture-in-a-small-cell situation to contend with. Like Leeuwenhoek, I hadn't been allowed a phone call, but unlike Leeuwenhoek this wasn't because Alexander Graham Bell was yet to invent the instrument. It was all down to the Moroccan Military, who, subcontracted by the CIA to interrogate terror suspects, felt they had to be a lot nastier than they would have been normally.

Denied food and water, and forced to watch a six-disc set of André Rieu DVDs, I was in understandably bad shape when Una turned up to bail me out. After the unfortunate Streisand incident, my agent had been banned from all international air travel and so had contacted my researcher to come and get me. A substantial bribe was paid, and as we drove in Una's beat-up rental from Morocco's notorious Zaki prison to the airport, I feasted greedily on dates and figs and watched the tumbledown houses that made up the town of Saleh whisk mercifully by.

Una, as always, was a supermodel of politeness and tact, saying nothing as her lunch disappeared down my eager gullet. She was also as generous as she was beautiful, although as she let me out at the airport terminal she told me that the bribe, the cost of the plane ticket and the car rental (including petrol) would come out of my advance, plus she was charging me overtime and per diems.

'No greater spur to finish my book, my sweet,' I said with a grateful smile as she slammed the door and tore off.

❧

My belongings had been returned by my captors, but as I went through the box at the desk of the LAX Lost Luggage Department, I discovered one glaring omission. While my wallet, my passport and my library cards were all there – the baggage receipts for the two coffins were not.

'I'm afraid there's nothing I can do about it, sir,' said the clerk, with the no-nonsense officiousness of someone trying to create the impression of doing all they can to help while, at the same time, not actually helping at all. 'No receipt, no bags. It's LAX policy.'

'It certainly is.'

'How's that, sir?'

'Lax policy.'

'I'm afraid I don't understand, sir.'

'LAX as in "lax".'

'I'm sorry, sir?'

True Anglo-sarcasm being lost on Americans, I changed direction but not subject. 'Is there someone else I could speak to, please?'

The clerk thought for a moment. 'There is the Executive Customer Liaison Manager, Carol Muskegan—'

'Ah – good,' I interrupted. I was a busy man; I had a 350-year-old corpse to revive and not a moment to lose. 'Fetch her at once.'

'Unfortunately … she's on her lunch break. She won't be back for half an hour.'

'Is that right?'

'Yes, sir.'

I drummed my fingers on the counter and gave an Oliver Hardyesque slow burn to the security camera in the corner of the ceiling.

'Then why mention her?' I sighed.

The clerk flashed a rhetorical smile and started chirping interminably in a language she'd learned from a manual. The upshot was that the CIA had got a hold of my coffins.

❧

IF YOU APPROACH THE CIA MEMORIAL Wall at their headquarters in Langley, Virginia, and press all eighty-nine stars in a certain sequence, the inch-thick plate of glass housing the Moroccan goatskin-bound 'Book of Honour' that juts out of the wall underneath will slide open. If you remove the book, you will see a small semicircular indentation in the base of the stainless-steel frame. If you then stand on your tip-toes, lean in and press your right eye to the indentation, a powerful infra-red camera will read the intricate structures of your iris and a computer will then turn this reading into a complex mathematical map. If this unique arrangement matches one of the four in the computer's memory, the wall will open and you will be able to descend a stone staircase into the highly secret Francis Gary Powers Room, named after the famous CIA U-2 spy-plane pilot, who, in 1960, heroically strayed into Soviet airspace and was shot down over Sverdlovsk.

Only the President of the United States, the Secretary of State, the current Director of Central Intelligence (Porter J. Gross) and the janitor have sufficient clearance to be in the room – and all four were gathered there at that moment, standing a respectful distance from the twin sarcophagi, the lids hovering overhead on taut suspension cables.

'What you are about to see, Mr President,' vouchsafed DCI Gross solemnly, 'will alter not only the course of human history, but also our ability to comprehend everything that has come before it.'

The President didn't understand what this meant but nodded anyway. He had another meeting in twelve minutes.

DCI Gross gestured to the President and Secretary of State that they come closer. The air was thick with anticipation as they peered into the first of the coffins.

Inside was the pale-faced young man I had discovered in the bowels of Midlothian's Lodge Rosslyn St Clair No. 606.

'Dead for 350 years but beautifully preserved,' declared Gross. He paused for a moment, his fingers to his pursed lips, before moving to the second sarcophagus. 'But it is the other, outwardly identical body that has caused us concern.'

'How so?' asked the Secretary of State, eager for a line.

The DCI leaned over and tapped the other pale-faced figure on the nose with his fingernail. A brittle *toc* was heard by all, even by the janitor, who was way over on the other side of the room, leaning on his mop. Brows furrowed in unison.

'Fibreglass,' announced the DCI. 'Painted to give an authentic skin tone. Of course, our scientists were able to spot the hoax almost immediately.'

'Are you sure?' enquired a sceptical President. 'Did you carbon date the material?'

'We did,' said the DCI with a wry smile. He'd been expecting the question. You didn't rise to the top of the CIA and remain there for almost three consecutive administrations without knowing one or two things about anticipating the next guy's move. 'It's a standard Tong Hua Display System Co. Ltd. mannequin, Model No. 102. No more than a year old. Customised, of course, by someone who knew what he was doing.'

The President glanced at his watch, clapped his hands and headed for the door. The Secretary of State handed the DCI her departmental business card and pointed to her deliberately incorrect mobile phone number on the back. 'Call me anytime,' she said as they left.

Gross smiled to himself, confident a Congressional Medal of Honour would be coming his way soon. The janitor, meanwhile, set to work removing the President's scuff marks.

Chapter 19

**IN WHICH THE RIPPER MEETS HIS MATCH
AND WORSE THINGS HAPPEN AT SEA**

*30th day of September Anno Domini Iesu Christi 1888,
22:55:21 post meridiem GMT, the northern banks of the Thames,
across from Rotherhithe, East London*

UBSEQUENT TO THE PREVIOUS meanwhile, most of the members of the Greater London constabulary had assembled and hidden themselves in and around the Limehouse docks, awaiting orders from Lestrade to flush out the Ripper Moray. Many were armed with freshly issued Lee-Metford repeating rifles, a first for the British police.

'All righ' then, Jack – we know you're in thar!' bellowed Lestrade through his bullhorn. 'Now, 'is you goin' to come along quie'ly? Or are we goin' to 'ave to use force?'

A crazed Moray flung open a window in the uppermost storey of the abandoned Chinese

*Then he threw his head back and
cackled like a maniac.*

laundry he was holed up in. He looked out over
the sea of bobby helmets beneath him, then
threw his head back and cackled like a maniac.

'I can take him out, Guv,' whispered PC
Abercrombie Jones, kneeling by Lestrade, his
rifle balanced on his crook'd arm, keen eye
squinting over the cocked hammer, his aim
fixed on the laughing Scotsman.

'Then do it,' hissed his superior.

The trigger was pulled, the hammer
obediently struck the firing pin, a clean shot

rang out and the glass in a nearby lamppost exploded.

Moray wheezed in the manner of Lou Costello[24] and quickly shut the window.

The PC immediately set about reading the 'How to Reload' section of the rifle's instruction booklet. Of course, it was a lot harder to read now there was less light.

'In the name of 'er Majesty Queen Victoria, I order you to yield!' Lestrade bellowed again. Then someone tugged at his sleeve.

'Let me have a word with him,' said Alexander Pruitt from his bath chair.

Lestrade wasn't so sure this was wise. 'I'm not so sure that would be wise,' he said, proving he was a man who knew his mind and made no secret of it.

'Let him at least talk to Moray,' urged Conan Doyle.

PC Abercrombie Jones pushed in the bolt on his rifle and inadvertently shot out another lamppost.

'Yes, please do,' concurred Wells.

---

24. Mayor of New York from 1934 to 1945 and famous for his enormous green beard. Ref. Wikipedia.

The Inspector's moustache twitched with indignation. 'This is a very dangerous situation—'

Three more lampposts were blown apart in rapid succession as some of the other constables joined in.

'Hold your fire!' Lestrade yelled through the bullhorn.

'Extraordinary times call for extraordinary measures, Inspector,' pleaded Conan Doyle. 'If I had told you a week ago that a 350-year-old dead man could be awakened, you would have taken me for a madman – but now you know it to be true!'

'And I know this Moray,' added Alexander.

'And *I* know that if this Moray should die tonight …' further added Sir Arthur, with his hand on Alexander's shoulder '… then so might this lad here.'

The Inspector eyed Conan Doyle levelly. 'How d'you mean?'

'Well, Doctor Moray is not murdering prostitutes for the sheer pleasure of it – he's murdering them as part of a series of medical experiments to see whether this fellow's genetic material can be successfully implanted into an unfertilised ovum. If you were to compare his DNA with that of the *foeti* removed from these poor women, you would see they are one and the same.'

Another lamppost was shot out, followed by a distant, 'Sor–ry!'

'Doctor Moray is laying the groundwork for the birth of young Master Pruitt here. If he doesn't arrange it by the year 1970, then Master Pruitt won't be born. Kill the Ripper, and Master Pruitt here will disappear in a puff of metaphorical smoke.'

'Like tears ... in the rain,' tacked on an increasingly redundant H. G. Wells.

Lestrade was so stunned that he didn't notice as several more lampposts were blasted to smithereens.

'But ... 'ow do you know all this?' he finally stammered.

Conan Doyle brandished a small piece of parchment and shook it under the Inspector's nose. 'It was all in this note pinned to Moray's chest when they revived him at the Lodge. It was in some seemingly impenetrable code, but after much study and with much patience, I have been able to decipher it. The science contained therein is much more advanced than anything known to modern medicine, all that business with "genes" and the like ... and to be honest with you, I have no idea what DNA is at all—'

The Inspector snatched the note from Conan Doyle and weighed up the situation as a Royal Artillery van pulled up. Attached to the roof was what appeared to be a Gatling gun. There were murmurs of approval from the multitude of bobbies.

'All righ', all righ',' said Lestrade, eager to avoid any further destruction of lampposts. 'He can speak to the Ripper for two minutes. *Two minutes.* Any longer, an' I order my men to move in.'

As Alexander Pruitt lifted himself from his bath chair and walked unsteadily towards the building that housed Mr Zhen's Authentic Chinese Laundry, the stony-faced Inspector glanced down at the fob watch he held in his increasingly trembling hand. It was two minutes to midnight.

✍

ALEXANDER PRUITT FOUND DR ROBERT
Fenwick Aloysius Moray to be quite reasonable,
in the circumstances. The Scot conceded that
things had got out of hand murder-wise, but
claimed that it wasn't actually his fault.

The doctor explained that a breakaway
faction within the Masons, keen that the
Monarchy be restored with the Catholic
bloodline of James II instead of his Protestant
brother, Charles II, had wanted Moray to fail
in his quest to prolong the life of the Protector-
Apparent, Richard, thus allowing James and his
King Louis XIV–supplied French mercenaries
to ride in and grab power from the ailing Oliver
Cromwell, instead of James having to wait to
inherit the Crown upon his brother's death.
With several extra decades to breed and produce
Catholic offspring, they reasoned, there would
never be any Glorious Revolution, never any
need for Mary and William of Orange, never
any rotten old Dutch House of Hanover, and,
thus, a much weaker British Parliament to deal
with in the future.

Jack the Ripper was therefore not a single
crazed lunatic after all, but a secret cabal of
right-wing Catholic Freemasons who had been

systematically murdering Moray's unwitting human cloning experiments for their own political ends. Catholics! The very last people Alexander Pruitt expected would be guilty of anything so twisted and diabolical – not counting Opus Dei.

But what of Sir Arthur's interpretation of the doctor's motives? Was Moray's masquerade as the Queen's chiropodist and his illicit impregnation of prostitutes in Victorian London really nothing more than an innocent ruse and rehearsal for implanting Richard Cromwell's DNA into Alexander's mother eighty-two years later?

Moray nodded.

'But surely,' reasoned Alexander, as he paced back and forth across the floor of the laundry's steam room, 'if my existence is entirely dependent on you cloning me from Richard Cromwell's DNA, then my existence equally depends on you murdering me when I visit your surgery in the year 2005 so that my soul is sent back to the seventeenth century to inhabit the body I now have.'

Doctor Moray thought a moment and then looked up. 'Yes, I suppose you're right. I hadn't actually thought of that. That complicates things a bit, doesn't it?'

'It does rather,' said Alexander morosely.

'I fear we're in something of an ontological cleft stick,' said Moray.

'In the meantime,' said Alexander, glancing at his wrist under the mistaken impression that his watch would be there, 'Lestrade and his men will storm this place in less than a minute to arrest you.'

At that very moment the skylight swung open and a long coil of hemp rope unfurled with a thump to the floor. Moray and Alexander looked up to see the grinning face of H. G. Wells peering over the transom.

'Climb up, *mon ami*,' invited the till now seemingly supernumerary author. 'There's a rowboat ready to take you to Calais. Our French brothers will see to it that you will be well hidden.'

Moray let out a triumphant bray of laughter and clasped Alexander by the arm. 'Then our sacred mission is saved. We'll see each other in a hundred years or so, my friend.'

'But wait—' begged an exasperated Alexander as the Scot shinnied up the cord with the expertise of a bilge rat. 'What do we do when we meet again in the year 2005?'

Doctor Moray swung his legs onto the rooftop and looked down on his young partner in Time. 'Well, there'll be two Alexander Pruitts – at least, until I have to murder one of you. Why not work it out between yourselves!'

And with that baffling piece of advice, he was gone.

❧

THE GREAT LIMEHOUSE LAUNDRY SIEGE of 1888 was over. After an alarmingly inaccurate display of Gatling gun marksmanship, in which most of Mr Zhen's Laundry survived largely unscathed, Alexander Pruitt was arrested and held on suspicion of aiding and abetting the escape of Jack the Ripper.

Mysteriously, no charges were ever laid. Masonic forces deep within the Halls of Justice, with tentacles reaching to the House of Lords itself, ensured the release that very day of young Alexander. The men of influence returned him to the care of Sir Arthur, who, in turn, delivered him into the hands of those in the Royal Society's Masonic elite who would send him safely back to his cold slumbers, and manifest destiny, somewhere in the knot of underground chambers of a secret Lodge hidden under Westminster Abbey.

H. G. Wells, meanwhile, fell into the English Channel on the way to France and drowned. As a result, all the stories he wrote between 1888 and 1941, including, ironically, *The Shape of Things to Come*, were never actually written.

Things like that happen when you muck about with Time.[25]

---

25. Of course, one of the good things to come out of all this was that because Wells never wrote it, Tom Cruise never ended up not making *War of the Worlds* (*cf.* Ch. 15).

Chapter 20

IN WHICH THE UNIVERSE IS DESTROYED

*14th day of January Anno Domini Iesu Christi 3050,
03:54:59 ante meridiem GMT, Outer Space*

N THE MOMENT THAT H. G. WELL'S novel *The Shape of Things to Come* suddenly ceased ever to have been written, something quite bizarre and wholly unexpected took place.

At first, it was hardly noticeable – in fact, Maurice Binns, astronomer at the Sphinx Observatory at Jungfraujoch in the Swiss Alps, almost missed it: a faint pulse of light in the middle of the curve of the Big Dipper, exactly midway between Arcturus and Boötes. Claude had been reaching for a bottle of slightly flat Pommac when he noticed the glimmer out of the corner of his eye.

The astronomer dutifully rang his supervisor,

who was at home in bed, to tell him all about it. The supervisor was so cross at having been woken up that he went back to sleep and did nothing about it. Not that there was anything that could have been done.

The pulse increased in intensity and frequency, sending out powerful electromagnetic waves. Pretty soon the seven stars that make up the popular Ursa Major constellation started to implode, in turn causing any planets orbiting these stars to hurtle off and collide with each other. Electromagnetic waves radiated out from this hub like the ripples in an otherwise placid lake, and star system after star system was snuffed out and broken up in an exponential chain reaction that, eventually, unravelled the very fabric of the Universe.

Half an attosec before, however – and quite coincidentally – a spaceship travelling through the iZwicky 18 Galaxy suddenly disappeared and then reappeared several million years earlier.

Inside the craft, Senior Detective Sergeant Zamelf cracked open his left eye; his right eye was still frozen shut.

He let his left eye dart about a bit.

His vision was unfocused and there was too much white light burning his brain.

His limbs ached.

Awake for less than thirty seconds and he was already tired.

'Are we there yet?' he croaked to no-one in particular.

Gradually the familiar shape of Una appeared out of the glare. Her voice was dead and reassuring.

'Sorry to bother you, Senior Detective Sergeant, but there is an emergency.'

❧

THE GREAT SPACESHIP GLIDING THROUGH the vast, yielding vacuum of space was the WF-G1700.

Deep within her cargo hold slept 100,000 creatures from across the reaches of the Universe, who had been charged with every crime imaginable and unimaginable. They had been frozen on arrest, pending trial upon their return to the thirteenth moon in the Kuiper Belt. The 100,000 alien beings and the paperwork their arrests had generated were all neatly filed away in the bowels of the massive spaceship that

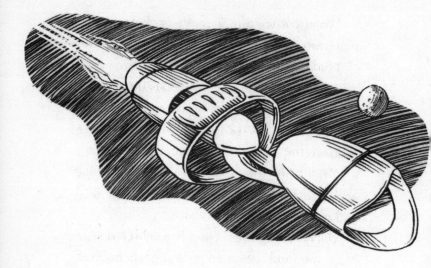

She was the WF-G1700.

operated as a watchhouse-cum-giant-police-station-cum-intergalactic-patrol wagon.

It had taken millions of years to track down these miscreant life forms. Of course, most of the original police squad had died; only Zamelf remained. The robot support staff – the Adminidroids™ – were doing their best to keep him alive until they got home, keeping him on ice for most of the time and only thawing him out in an emergency.

The last time they'd woken him was three thousand years ago, when a rogue Otanian borg

had been cornered in a crater on Palaxan-90,
an unmoored ghetto station floating in the
Manteda System. Zamelf had read him
his rights through the WF-G1700 tannoy,
and then dropped back to sleep before the
Adminidroids™ had immersed the screaming
borg in the vat of pre-cryogenic delousing
solution – which was, it must be said, freaking
cold.

This time it wasn't an arrest.

The Adminidroids™, who had achieved self-
awareness and begun replicating themselves
millions of years ago, were a very efficient
society. They ran the WF-G1700 as a very
tight ship. All the Adminidroids™ were exact
copies of Una, who had originally been placed
on board as a sort of back-up file server-cum-
pleasure-model. Now, through her manifold
emissaries, she ran the place.

As all the Adminidroids™ looked, sounded
and acted like Una, Zamelf found it easier
to address whichever Adminidroid™ he
happened to be talking to as Una, and as all the
Adminidroids™ shared a single type of wireless
consciousness, whichever one he was talking to
regarded herself as Una.

The only thing Una could not do was repair the ship's HyperTime G-Tor®, which had broken down several million years ago. The WF-G1700 couldn't get home without it, and so continued patrolling its beat, arresting criminals, freezing them and storing them in its apparently limitless supply of gaol cylinders.

'When you say an "emergency",' yawned Zamelf hopefully, 'I take it you're not referring—'

'To the HyperTime G-Tor®?' said Una, efficiently, and annoyingly, completing Zamelf's question. 'Yes, I'm not.'

It took Zamelf's foggy oblongata a few moments to untangle what he was being told, by which time he was being wheeled on a gurney into the ship's observatory. His body was seized up, although the needle Una had given him was having an effect: a calming warmth was spreading through his body and he found he could now wiggle his toes without cramping and feeling spasms up his legs. His hands were useless, though, still clawed and numb, cupped on the pillow near his head.

An hour later, and Zamelf could sit up unaided. Una had brewed him a reasonable facsimile of hot cocoa and he huddled over the mug, taking in its reassuring aroma. It took him back to Earth, the sweetness and warmth conjuring up memories of his kitchenette and, more specifically, his wife, Jasmine, on the day he left home.

Zamelf closed his eyes and sucked in the steaming brew. The smell and taste of hot cocoa was all he had left of Jasmine; she and several hundred thousand generations of her ancestors would be long buried by now, natural processes reducing them, combined, to a jerry can of unleaded.

Una wanted Zamelf to look at what they'd picked up through the ship's TelemetriScope™. Archaic in design, the TelemetriScope™ was essentially eight ginormous telescopes welded together. The WF-G1700's Octnocular TelemetriScope™ (aka OtiS™) combined the messages from all eight radio mirrors to simulate a single larger, but condensed, telescope. OtiS™ was randomly trained by a computer with shifting coordinates to capture images from space, in the hope that it would record what the old terrestrial astronomers called 'First Light' – basically, the Birth of the Universe.[26]

Getting your coordinates would obviously be easier if the HyperTime G-Tor® was operational, because you could then hop back in time to an exact distance – but because someone spilled coffee on it just before 4 am on a January day in AD 3050, the WF-G1700 could no longer hop, with any certainty, from one strand of the space-time continuum to another. Thus far, in several million years of looking and several quintillion gigabytes of hard-drive recording data, they'd had no luck catching the actual Birth of the Universe.

---

26. Light travels at a speed of 1,079,252,848.8 km/h, which means that if you were 1,079,252,848.8 km away when the Universe started existing, it would take an hour before you noticed it. As the Universe is, at the time of writing, about 14 billion years old and light travels only 9,460,730,472,580.8 km in a Julian calendar year, you have to be quite some distance away in order to see the Universe being given birth to. The difficulty with this is that the Universe is constantly expanding (156 billion light years wide and counting), so it's a bit tricky to get your bearings. Essentially, though – get far enough away and you can take a pretty impressive picture of the Big Bang.

Instead, the Adminidroids™ had been using OtiS™ to snoop on history.

They'd recorded everything from the Destruction of Gliese 580 and the Attack of the Argalla Beast (Epsilon Eridani), right through to the Kennedy Assassination (Earth) and even 55 Cancri's failed attempt to restart its planetary core.

Zamelf himself had witnessed the Kennedy Assassination and, after the wrongful arrest of Lee Harvey Oswald, had decided to intervene. Unfortunately, sending down a replicant humanoid called Jack Ruby only confused matters and so, a thousand or so years later, Zamelf arrived on Earth and, under the cover of darkness, arrested Kaggalon Cotex (aka Mrs Jeanne Nusbaum), a large tripe-like creature running a dry cleaning business in Hoboken, New Jersey, by day, and at night secretly fronting an Upsilon Andromedae terrorist cell plotting the overthrow of the Earth's governments.

Thanks to the vigilance of the crew of the WF-G1700, the Upsilon plan to dominate the planet and enslave humankind never came to pass. However, this was in fact the last time the WF-G1700 got to use the HyperTime G-Tor®. During the onboard freezing process, Kaggalon Cotex got loose from the cryobay, and in the scuffle that ensued one of his tentacles towel-flicked Acting Lieutenant Marp right in the cods.

At that point – exactly 3.55 am – as Acting Lieutenant Marp involuntarily folded over in pain, his head came into sharp contact with a tray of refreshments held by one of the Unas. The computer got spattered with coffee, the drive shorted out, the HyperTime G-Tor® suffered a power surge and the WF-G1700 suddenly jumped the space-time continuum by several million years.

And the spacecraft had continued to do this, moving backwards and forwards in time over the trillennia without warning, every three weeks or so. As a result, no-one on board knew where – or when – the hell they were.

But that's not the most extraordinary thing that happened.

Chapter 21

**IN WHICH THE LOCH NESS
MONSTER IS EXPLAINED**

⁓

*14th day of January Anno Domini Iesu Christi 3050,
03:53:57 ante meridiem GMT, Outer Space*

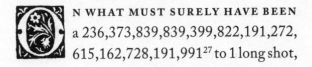 N WHAT MUST SURELY HAVE BEEN
a 236,373,839,839,399,822,191,272,
615,162,728,191,991[27] to 1 long shot,

---

27. 922,637,251,627,394,873,625,241,325,374,849,303,
838,373,636,363,636,363,636,363,738,392,020,109,162,
534,252,637,383,948,746,245,242,639,928,372,635,242,
525,266,371,819,287,373,948,373,625,263,732,929,378,
373,922,637,251,627,394,873,625,241,325,374,849,303,
838,373,636,363,636,363,636,363,738,392,020,109,162,
534,252,637,383,948,746,245,242,639,928,372,635,242,
525,266,371,819,287,373,948,373,625,263,732,929,378,
373,922,637,251,627,394,873,625,241,325,374,849,303,
838,373,636,363,636,363,636,363,738,392,020,109,162,
534,252,637,383,948,746,245,242,639,928,372,635,242,
525,266,371,819,287,373,948,373,625,263,732,929,378,
373,922,637,251,627,394,873,625,241,325,374,849,303,
838,373,636,363,636,363,636,363,738,392,020 recurring.

the WF-G1700, upon its sudden reappearance, pulled up alongside itself – that is to say, the WF-G1700, as it is now, happened across itself as it existed in a previous time. Una could tell it was a previous time, because she did a quick scan of the hull and determined that inside there were a great many more carbon-based life forms than they had had on board for a while now. Also, she had just seen an Arrest Pod fuse onto the Entry Bay and a manacled Kaggalon Cotex being escorted on board by several Adminidroids™.

It was AD 3050 at 03:53:57 am, and there wasn't a moment to lose – a point she thought she made rather neatly by spinning her head 180 degrees to face Zamelf and speaking in a higher register than usual.

'If we can get on board and prevent Acting Lieutenant Marp being hit in the cods, then the HyperTime G-Tor® will not be damaged.'

It was a temporal conundrum not unlike that faced by – and, as it would turn out, not wholly unconnected with – Alexander Pruitt. If a future event changes a past event, which, were it not for the future event, would have led to the future event in the first and second place, what happens instead?

'If we undo the event that resulted in us returning to the past, won't that mean we'll cease to exist?' asked Zamelf with surprising clarity, given that his brain was still a bit frozen.

Una, with maddening of-courseness, had already considered this. 'We would only cease to exist if we were our *future selves*. As we are our *current selves*, albeit *from* the future, we risk erasing nothing but past events.'

'Won't it be confusing if we board our own vessel?' asked Zamelf, his brow creased like a church bulletin on a hot day. 'I mean … we – though current versions of ourselves – will be confronting our past selves and … then …' He didn't know what he was talking about.

'Our past selves will be preoccupied with the escape of Kaggalon Cotex,' Una explained patiently. 'All we need to do is stop Acting Lieutenant Marp from entering the cryobay and getting his cods walloped.'

'Then what?'

'Then the HyperTime G-Tor® on *this* version of the WF-G1700 will once again become operational and we will be able to travel into the future – and then home …'

Home.

Zamelf could barely conceal his joy. He let out a yelp and kissed Una full on the lips. She was pretty damn sexy for a robot.

Just then another Una turned from the OtiS™ eyepiece, and said, 'We'd better hurry.'

Approximately 200,000 light years away in the Milky Way, on a small greeny-blue oblate spheroid orbiting a dying star, in a small body of land in a small grouping of buildings and roads, in an even smaller doctor's surgery, an incident was taking place that would start the hitherto-mentioned ripple across the space-time continuum; a ripple that would turn into a tear and eventually snuff out the Universe.

Una had traced the first inklings of that ripple back to the event they were in the process of observing, although the event itself had, of course, taken place 200,000 years earlier.

She'd tried to sort it out herself by popping down to earth a few times and interceding, but the closest she'd got was the day *after* the murder, when she got me involved.

❧

THE FIRST RULE OF TIME TRAVEL IS THAT you don't interfere with past or future events lest you cock things up (for example, by killing your grandfather and marrying your granddaughter etc) and create a Time Paradox. Unfortunately, no-one seems to obey this particular rule, and police throughout several galaxies have spent most of their time going backwards and forwards fixing things up – usually by arresting the time traveller *before* they travel forwards or backwards in time.

This could be very confusing for the would-be time traveller, who really hadn't done anything wrong when they were set upon, arrested and charged with the ultra-crime of 'Endangering the Very Existence of the Universe Itself'. Chances were he, she or it hadn't even thought of committing the crime in question.

As a result, Time Travel was eventually outlawed (that then became the First Rule and the original First Rule became the Second Rule), and the Third Rule decreed that only the police could use Time Travel, and even then only to effect an arrest *after* a crime had been committed, and even then only if and when the offending being had somehow escaped the meting out of justice by the species to which the said offending being belonged.

There was also a Fourth Rule, which said that the police could use Time Travel to 'arrest *before* a crime was committed but only where the crime in question was a Time Crime and where that Time Crime imperilled the Existence of the Universe Itself'.

Such was the case now, according to Una.

It was therefore fortuitous that the damaged WF-G1700 had come across an earlier and fully operational version of itself, because Zamelf could now go back in time and stop Alexander Pruitt being murdered by Doctor Moray, thereby preventing the start of the ripple, et cetera, et cetera, et cetera.

Fortuitous, that is, until the fully operational version of the WF-G1700 started firing on its damaged future self.

An explosion tore through the fuselage and a barrage of plasma bolts took their deadly toll on the hull. Zamelf barked at Una to radio the disarm code and slammed himself into the perspex Displacement Booth. But the damage was done; the future WF-G1700 was crippled and the temperature in the thermonuclear reactor was fast approaching vapour point.

Zamelf beamed himself aboard the WF-G1700 of the past. Una was already there, having replaced the ether-circuits of the older Unas on board, but no amount of explaining could stop them firing on their future selves.

In the ensuing panic, Acting Lieutenant Marp was kicked in the groin, and as he doubled up in pain he banged his head on a drinks tray, which splattered the computer. The spaceship hopped a few time frames forwards and backwards and then vanished, proving that Destiny is more about where you end up than the journey you might take to get there.

❧

KAGGALON COTEX MANAGED TO CLAMBER onto the outside of the WF-G1700 as it hurtled towards Earth. Her fur burned off upon entering the atmosphere and she fell, perplexed, into the cooling waters of Loch Ness as the mother ship broke up and an escape saucer headed for a crashlanding on the other side of the globe,

*Her fur burned off upon entering the atmosphere and
she fell into the cooling waters of Loch Ness.*

a few thousand kilometres from Scotland,
somewhere near Roswell, New Mexico.

As a child walking to school in Birmingham,
Charlie Pruitt had noticed a light streaking
across the sky. He thought it was a comet
at the time, and now has only a very vague
memory of it.

Chapter 22

8th day of March Anno Domini Iesu Christi 2005,
09:12:39 ante meridiem GMT, Camden St Egham, Kent

LEXANDER PRUITT HAD ASKED Sir Arthur Conan Doyle to arrange that the Rogerites wake him two weeks earlier than the day of his murder so he could think of a way out of his dilemma.

The way he looked at it, there were two choices.

If he stopped Moray murdering his 2005 self, then Richard Cromwell would die in 1657 and Alexander's 1657 self would suddenly and simultaneously cease to exist in the year 2005.

On the other hand, if Alexander didn't stop Moray from murdering his 2005 self, then Richard Cromwell would live and Alexander would have slept through the last couple of centuries for nothing. Plus, there would now be two Alexander Pruitts occupying the same temporal plane, so he could never go back to his old life.

Alexander hot-footed it over to his father's place and, using the spare key under the garden gnome, let himself in. Quite rightly feeling that his Cromwellian garb would arouse suspicions, he borrowed some of his own clothes, even miraculously finding the jumper he thought he'd lost.

He grabbed some loose cash his dad always kept in a jar above the stove, made a sandwich, and then caught a bus to the other side of town, where he lay low until the day of his medical appointment with Doctor Moray.

He'd decided against meeting with himself beforehand, thinking that would be confusing for both of him. He'd also decided not to confront his father, for fear he'd squeal to Moray. Instead, Alexander thought the best approach would be to burst in on Moray's examination and see what happened.

Maybe Moray wouldn't be able to go through with the murder. Sure, Alexander would then cease to exist, but at least he'd still be around in his 2005 form. He wouldn't know what he knew now but maybe it would be better that he never knew what he had learned. Or something.

If Moray did murder him, maybe he could tell himself what had happened in his final moments. He liked that idea. Very noble.

Either way, Alexander wouldn't be able to stop one or other of him (hopefully, not both) ceasing to exist. He resolved that if it were his soul that was returned to the seventeenth century, he would make sure Richard Cromwell stayed where he was and became Lord Protector; otherwise, the cycle would keep repeating, and he'd spend the rest of his existence being reborn and murdered 350 years later.

Of course, he couldn't stop the year 2005 Alexander from doing exactly what he'd ended up doing, travelling across the centuries to prevent his murder. But that was the natural order of things. Or as much as they could be.

⤶

ALEXANDER RODE THE ANTIQUE ELEVATOR up to Moray's rooms. The woman behind the desk gave him a bemused look of the type Cary Grant used to specialise in.

'I thought you just went in,' she said to him as he strode past.

'Déjà vu,' Alexander offered unconvincingly, opening the door to the surgery and slipping in as unobtrusively as a doppelganger can.

A startled Doctor Moray swung around. So did the equally startled 2005 version of himself. The 1657 version of himself was expecting this but what he wasn't expecting was to see a third person in the room – particularly when that third person was also himself.

'Huh?' he posited, startled.

The third version of Alexander Pruitt was standing next to Doctor Moray, trying to wrestle away the large syringe filled with a glittering turquoise solution. He paused momentarily in order to be startled as well.

'Who the hell are you?' asked the third version of Alexander of the 1657 version of Alexander.

'What do you mean "Who the hell am I?" – who the hell are you?'

'Isn't that my jumper?' queried the original Alexander (if, indeed, there was an original Alexander) from his seat.

'Isn't that my jumper?' queried the original Alexander.

'You see, I told you it was pointless trying to stop me,' said Moray. 'It's all pre-ordained. You're just making it worse.'

All three Alexanders were as one in not knowing what the doctor was talking about. But for different reasons.

'Don't you see?' he continued, pushing away the restraining hand of the third Alexander and standing closer to the window, so he could be framed by curtains and create a more appropriate setting for a denouement. 'Despite your best efforts to stop me killing you, I inevitably succeed – as evinced by the fact that you turn up, yet again, to stop me.'

The third Alexander paused a moment to take this in.

'Right,' he said eventually. 'So, you end up murdering me, sending my soul back to the seventeenth century and then I, as Richard Cromwell, travel into the future via suspended animation to prevent the murder—'

'Only you fail,' continued the 1657 Alexander, warming to the subject. 'The original version of me—'

'Us,' corrected the third Alexander.

'Us …' conceded the 1657 Alexander. 'The original version of *us* dies and his soul goes back again, and then I put myself into suspended animation for three hundred-odd years, and turn up to try to prevent the murder as well—'

'I don't understand,' offered the original, and completely dumbfounded, Alexander.

The other two Alexanders looked at each other, as if in unspoken understanding of a slightly dimmer younger brother.

'No, no – hear me out,' pleaded the original Alexander, not unreasonably. 'Wouldn't I realise if I were one of you, that this had already happened—'

He had something there, but there was barely enough time to consider what it was before a fourth version of Alexander bolted through the door.

'What the freak—' he began.

'I think we are caught in some sort of temporal loop,' explained Doctor Moray, at which point a fifth version of Alexander entered the room. 'I think the only way out of it is to *not* commit the murder.'

'Then we will cease to exist because we were never sent back to become Richard Cromwell,' surmised either the second or third Alexander – it was getting hard to tell.

'You can tell by the jumper,' explained the original Alexander, in a narrative impossibility that, while audaciously deconstructive, did rather reek of desperation in a novel's closing moments.

'The only way we can prevent the continuing multiplicity of Alexander Pruitts entering my surgery—' and a sixth, seventh and eighth version wandered in as if to underline the point, 'is for me to resolve *not* to save the life of Richard Cromwell by sending the soul of his clone back 350 years.'

'Well, can you hurry up and not do it,' asked the second Alexander plaintively, 'it's getting crowded in here.'

A ninth, tenth and eleventh version of Alexander appeared at the door, as did Moray's harried receptionist.

'Doctor Moray, I'd like to give my notice …' Behind her, several more Alexanders could be seen trying to get in the door.

Moray looked at his watch. Unless he administered the fatal injection to the year 2005 Alexander in the next seven seconds, the two ages would not identically correspond and the soul transference would fail. He stood back and folded his arms.

    Six.

    Five.

    Four.

    Three.

    Two.

This was it. The Alexander wearing his favourite jumper wondered for a moment whether history would judge him harshly if, in a last, frantic moment of self-preservation, he leaned over and plunged the fatal needle into the yielding neck of the original Alexander himself.

But what would it accomplish? More and more Alexanders were gathering in the waiting room, which had become some sort of temporal nexus gridlock. He resolved to do nothing and see what would happen.

One.

There was a wink in time and Doctor Moray's surgery was bathed in a magenta hue. Then all the Alexander Pruitts vanished but for the original.

The receptionist, though, still insisted on handing in her resignation.

∽

LATER THAT AFTERNOON, ALEXANDER turned up at the Fox and Grapes to find his father in deep conversation with me. The old man was so pleased to see him. There were hugs. Beers were consumed and outlandish stories were told. There was even talk of the need to make a mannequin and take it on holiday to Scotland. The old man put it down to some new medication Alexander was taking, but agreed to do it.

I never did get to go on my adventure. Which is a great pity, because I think it would have made an interesting book. Instead, with the help of Una, I wrote an investigative piece for *Omni* about badgers and why they vanished from Europe at the turn of the century. We also wrote a novel together called *The Shape of Things to Come*, which did very nicely in the bestseller lists. Una says she has plenty more ideas like that.

We eventually married, Una and I. Would we last? Well, that was anyone's guess. Gaff had seen her; four years, he figured.

He was wrong. Tyrell had told me Una was special: no termination date. I didn't know how long we had together. Who does?

Acknowledgements

HANKS TO FRAN BERRY AT HGB for liking this book enough to publish it; to Project Manager Tracy O'Shaughnessy for her steadfast stewardship, guidance and encouragement; and to Editor Janet Austin for her manifold improvements to the text, many of which masked my poor command of the English language. Grammar, punctuation, spelling and structuring my thoughts in a coherent manner have never been my strong suits, and any lapses in these areas should be put down to my dogged insistence on retaining something despite sensible urging to alter it. Thanks also to Peter Long for his excellent design and to Bill Woods for his superb illustrations.

Thanks as well to my friends Mark O'Loughlin, Tony Martin and Sarina Rowell, who read early drafts and offered helpful advice.

While I'm at it, thanks to Mum and Dad, who convinced me I could achieve anything in this life, despite palpable evidence to the contrary.

And, finally, I acknowledge my eternal debt to my wife, Leandra.

Recommended reading

If you enjoyed reading this book, you may also enjoy:

Being Hit on the Head by A. Hammer

The Great Big Book of Mitochondria
by Steve and Celia Hunt

Scrimshaw Now! by Stacey Ahern

Knitting with Toffee by Kurt Andronicus

Sink Your Own Lusitania by Barry Ng

Calisthenics for Bees by Fiorello

Optional Gargling by O. Wilson Lockerby

An Open Letter to Robots by Alan Alda

Ridding Your Home of Glitter by Ronnie Cheeseman

*Minutes of the Third International Convention
on 'Kicking Mars' Ass!'* (various authors)

The Joy of Mannum by Dickie Chocolate

1000 Ways to Scotchgard Your Horse by Rick Tjaden

MENSA Squids edited by Emile Sitka

Chasing the Dream: Forging the Perfect Speculum
by Deepak Armstrong

Return Policy at the Tyrell Corporation
by J. F. Sebastian and Hannibal Chew

Pickling Eggs in the 1900s by Moms Mabely

Robert Menzies, Alien edited by Gareth Evans

Fashion During the Irish Potato Famine
by Seamus O'Hehir

Yo, Ancient and Modern: Hymns for Young People
by Ted Tinling

The Problem with Ghee by L. 'No Nickname' Sweeney
(unpublished manuscript)

I Made a Hearing Aid for Jerry Lewis's Dog
by Dr A. Q. Nesbitt

Highlights in Australian Television Comedy
by Balthazar Reed (pamphlet)

The How and Why Wonder Book of Swimming Pool Ghosts
by Malcolm Foote Jnr

Ancient Map Folding by Timmy Artemis

The Complete Book of Promite narrated by Cate Blanchett
(2 CD set)

Who's Who in Goth Porn by Pat Sullivan

Gas Pressure Readings in Adelaide, June–July 1934
by Driller Jet Aldrin

Bogan Christ-Child by Vulnavia Spratt

Why Things Sometimes Smell by Lolita Cattermole

If Dolphins Could Pilot Commercial Jets: A Reimagining of
9/11 by Lt. Commander Billy 'Tea' Hecuba

Babies Who Can Operate TiVo by Nina Krill

Are Volcanos Out to Get Us? and Other Dialogues about Conspiracy Geology by Professor Kat Bellnap

The Don Explains the Koran
by The Don Bradman Foundation

A Quick Badness
by Eunice M. Belsize (writing as Ian Fleming)

The Spanish Influenza Touch and Feel Book
by Laura Ortega and Morris To (Illustrator)

James Cyril Stobie, Telephone Pole Visionary or Nutball?
by Alex Ward

One Leg, One Dog and I Still Won the Iditarod
by Ray Milquetoast (as told to Brandi Flowers)

Tedious Stories about Tennis by Todd Woodbridge

Cult Leadership and How to Get the Permits
by Sally and Tim Birchall

Peat: The Forgotten Non-renewable Fuel by George Gipe

Tractors by Oliver Stone

Famous Prison Escape Movie Sheet Music
compiled by Anton Enus

Gay Malta by L. Zebedee Muscat

Rural Postmen Struck by Lightning by Gearóid McCaffrey

Was Tin Tin Burmese? by Fr. Abraham Simile

What Time is it in Greenland? 1770-1992 by Anonymous

Storming the Bastille: Why it Wouldn't Work in Space
by Alan Spoof

Coming soon

We Don't Need No Stinking Badgers
by Shaun Micallef

Why did badgers die out? Were they ever here? Did we *really* evolve from them? A delightful retelling of the famous Scope's Badger trial in 1925. Includes not only a full court transcript and hundreds of illustrations and photographs, but several lines of actual text by Micallef.

At AU$60.00, it's quite expensive.

'A tour de force'. The Age

Possum-proofing the Poetry
by Shaun Micallef

Move over A. D. Hope, there's a new kid in the hood and he wants to bust a rhyme in your ass.

Yes, having set the world of prose on fire with his debut best-seller, Preincarnate, the man Meanjin called 'repeatedly on the phone to get some back issues paid for' returns with a bucket of petrol and a match to burn down everything you thought you ever knew about poetry. Les Murray said 'it'll blow your mind' – mind you, he was talking about Avatar. Here is an excerpt:

A poet who came from the Rhine
Did not find it easy to rhyme
He started off well
But by the end you could tell
He'd lost interest in the whole thing and wasn't even
bothering with meter.

AU$80.00 (25% off if unautographed)

'A tour de force'. The Age

My Nightmare Life as a Crackhead
by Shaun Micallef

A blistering no-holds-barred account of Micallef's hellish excursion into the dark world of showbiz tell-all memoir. Micallef's drug addiction, alcoholism and battle with life-threatening illnesses are dealt with, as are his many infidelities and doomed marriage to Ukrainian PM, Yulia Tymoshenko. Told with a candour and sensitivity not often seen in cheap ghost-written autobiographies, this is a book the whole family should read (at the same time, so each member of the family will have to buy an individual copy).

AU$49.95

'A tour de force'. The Age

The Silly Adventures of Rodney the Horse
by Shaun Micallef

An enchanting children's fable about a horse called Rodney and the trouble he gets into trying to travel across Australia to visit his uncle. Written by Micallef in twenty minutes while waiting for a train, this book is a much-needed addition to the already groaning shelves of careless, celebrity-penned kids' books.

AU$24.95.

'A tour de France'. The Age